FAIRDAY MORROW
~ and the ~
Talking Library

JESSICA HAIGHT & STEPHANIE ROBINSON

Illustrations by DAVID SANANGELO

WILLOW PRESS

Visit us on the web: willowpress.org
Teachers and librarians learn more at: fairdaysfiles.com

Haight, Jessica.
The Talking Library/ Jessica Haight and Stephanie Robinson
- First Edition
pages cm.
Summary: The Detective Mystery Squad tries to stop a bookworm from eating words in stories. The mystery unwinds as the three sleuths uncover a world where books are born and legends guard a library that doesn't exist.

Library of Congress Control Number: 2017914080

ISBN 978-0-9993449-0-3 (hardback)—ISBN 978-0-9993449-2-7 (ebook)

ISBN 978-0-9993449-1-0 (paperback)

The text of this book is set in 12- point Times New Roman
Jacket design by Chris Robinson
Interior Design by Jessica Haight & Stephanie Robinson

10 9 8 7 6 5 4 3 2 1
First Edition

To Allison,
Truth Lies Betwixt the Lines.

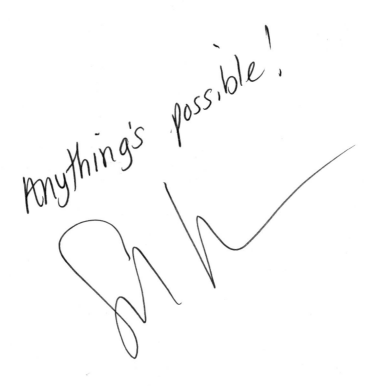

To my mom, and all the readers who like to connect the dots.

—J.H

To everyone who asked for the second book!

—S.R.

Anything's possible!

Lion: Yesterday I was lying.

Unicorn: So was I.

— Alice and Wonderland

(*Through the Looking Glass*)

ASHPOT WEEKLY

VOLUME 7, ISSUE 348 THURSDAY, AUGUST 27, 2015

BEGONIA ESTATE DONATES RARE PRIVATE COLLECTION

by Richard Bittner

Local librarians were shocked to find out that a collection of rare artifacts, owned by deceased recluse Thurston Begonia, will be donated to the Ashpot Library. Attorneys handling the estate informed library officials that the Begonia House was sold and certain things had to go. Rumors that the Begonia family had been cursed are well known in Ashpot, and this latest development has raised eyebrows with local residents. In life, Thurston Begonia was a noted treasure hunter, but after his only daughter, Ruby, disappeared on her wedding day, he stayed out of the public eye. Given suspicions surrounding the manner of his death, folks in Ashpot have voiced their concerns over what the library may have inherited from the infamous Begonia House. No doubt, its secrets will be spilled soon enough. The list of items hasn't been released to the public yet, but once the contents of this valuable donation have been thoroughly reviewed, Thurston Begonia's private collection will be open for viewing.

⁓ One ⁓
STRANGE NOTES

Fairday Morrow woke to a loud crack of thunder. As she bolted upright in bed, her gray eyes flew open. Rain pelted against the window. Electricity charged the air. Lightning flashed, and she saw the old willow tree in her backyard lurching wildly. A whip-like branch smashed the glass and the storm raged into her room. BOOM! The sky lit up. The wind blew in like a tornado, tossing wet leaves and sticks around. Fairday shrieked and ducked under the covers.

"Fairday! Are you okay?" her dad shouted from the hallway.

Auntie Em, the family pug, was barking her head off.

"Yeah, I'm alright," Fairday answered in a shaky voice. She peeked out from the blankets as a burst of light split the dark.

For an instant, glass shards twinkled like stars across the tattered lion-and-unicorn carpet; the heavy drapes flapped, twisting in the wind. On the next lightning strike, Fairday saw a paper blow in through the broken window. But the second she glimpsed it, thunder boomed, the house shook, and everything blacked out.

Her dad appeared in the doorway with a flashlight, and Fairday spotted the paper by her feet. Snatching it with fingertips, she leaped from bed and followed the beam of light to safety, careful not to tread on the glittering rug.

Mr. Morrow set up a sleeping area in the parlor, and Fairday climbed onto the couch, keeping the note hidden up her pajama sleeve. The Begonia House Bed and Breakfast was still under construction, so the space wasn't luxurious. Sheets speckled with dried paint covered the knotted wood floors and ladders leaned against ceiling-high bookshelves cloaked in blue tarps. An enormous stone fireplace with a blanket stretched over the opening sucked in and out from the draft, and the air had a confusing blend of odors, sort of a sanitized mustiness. Progress was being made, but Fairday could feel her mom shudder every time a layer of wallpaper was peeled away, only to reveal another gaudy pattern to unstick.

Raising an eyebrow, Mr. Morrow sat down and tugged
Fairday's ponytail. "You okay? You look pale."

"I always do." Fairday shrugged and felt the note crinkle
against her skin. She gave her dad a small smile. "Really,
I'm fine."

Mr. Morrow cast a tall shadow on the wall as he stood
up. He ran a hand through his messy black hair, a trait
she'd inherited. "Well, it seems like everything that can
go wrong has. But that's change for you. Best to work
the kinks out now."

"I guess," Fairday said. Her parents' dream to restore this
crumbling Victorian into a bed and breakfast had inspired
their recent move from Manhattan to Ashpot, Connecticut.

3

Fairday thought starting fifth grade at the end of September had been rough, but fixing this place was turning out to be a real pain for her parents.

"That's my girl. Sleep tight." He winked, then turned to leave.

"Dad?"

"Yes?"

"Are you and Mom happy you bought the Begonia House?" Fairday had to know. She *did not* want to move again. Just yesterday, her parents had argued over a repair bill. She'd even heard her dad say that cobwebs must be the only thing keeping this place together. Fairday could tell her parents were stressed, and her little sister, Margo, hadn't been making it easier. Not by her own fault—she just wasn't going to stop being a two-year-old anytime soon.

Mr. Morrow sighed. "After Livingston Prep closed, and I lost my job, it felt like the time was right for Mom and me to follow our passions. Bringing the Begonia House back to life is a golden opportunity. With her interior design skills and my wizardry in the kitchen, we'll make our dream tangible." He opened his arms to the room. "So, yes, we're happy. There are always going to be challenges, Fairday. Remember what I told you about roadblocks?"

"That they're there for a reason?" Fairday answered. Even though her dad wasn't the head of an English department anymore, he could never resist a teachable moment. It was why she had such a good vocabulary.

"Correct!" Mr. Morrow spun on his heels. "If there aren't twists and turns in the road, the drive's a bore. G'night, m'lady." Tipping an imaginary hat, he shut the door.

Snuggling into the blankets, Fairday thought about his words. Living here definitely wasn't boring. The Begonia House was full of surprises. It was even famous in Ashpot because of the tragedies and speculation surrounding the Begonia family. Kids in school kept asking about it, so her parents agreed she could throw a Halloween party. She and Lizzy had come up with the idea for a "boo—k" themed party. Even though she had concerns about people poking around her house, she thought it *would* be interesting to see all the costumes. You could tell a lot about a person based on the story character they chose to be. Fairday felt her nerves flutter at the thought of her classmates coming over. What would they think of the cracked walls and slanted hallways? Hopefully, it would add to the spooktacularness.

Sliding the paper out of her sleeve, Fairday read the note. The message was disturbing. Even stranger, it wasn't the first she'd found. It was the third in a week, and they all said the same thing.

> **The Librarian has been double-crossed. Many words will be lost. Lest the bookworm goes away, story ink is how books pay. We seek the one who wears the shoes—only they can hear the news.**

Fairday wished she understood the riddle. Who was the Librarian? How were words lost? *What* was a bookworm? She thought of her favorite stories, and her heart fell, imagining a world where they didn't exist. Fairday *did not* want words to vanish and vowed to solve the mystery.

She and her best friend, Lizzy Mackerville, started the Detective Mystery Squad, also known as the DMS, in third grade. They'd solved a couple of cases after that, but nothing like the recent investigation of Ruby Begonia, the missing bride. She'd disappeared from the Begonia House on her wedding day, over fifty years ago. No one had a clue what happened to her until the DMS uncovered evidence that led them to a parallel world on the other side of the Begonia House. They'd found Ruby trapped in time there, cursed by a gypsy named Eldrich. The enchantment was broken when she gave Lizzy bright red high-heeled flying sneakers. They not only ended the spell, but now her friend owned magical shoes! Whoever sent the message must be looking for Lizzy, but why could she hear the news? Did the sneakers have more powers to reveal?

Fairday had found the first note a few days ago. It'd been left as a bookmark in her favorite book, *The Wizard of Oz*, which she always kept on her nightstand. She was surprised that a passage she knew by heart had changed. When the Tin Woodman said, "Brains do not make one happy, and happiness is the best thing in the world," happy and happiness were gone. Instead, it read, "Brains do not make one, and is the best thing in the world." How could this book, which had been passed down from her grandmother, be missing words, like they'd never been there at all? Realizing the warning could be more worrisome than she'd thought, Fairday's stomach clenched.

Another note appeared a few days later while Fairday was fixing up the secret room on the third floor as DMS headquarters (Ruby's old bedroom). When she was organizing her desk, she'd heard a crash. Her backpack had fallen off the table, and the fingerprinting powder had smashed open. She'd found the second note in the jar while cleaning up the mess. Fairday had emailed Lizzy about it, and they'd concluded that the pack must have tipped off the table. But where did the note come from? Ruby said she'd been trapped alone on the other side of the house all those years. Was it possible that someone else was stuck there too?

Fairday began to drift off when she noticed a large spider crawl out of a crack in the wall. "Hello, spider," she said. Normally, she'd have been creeped out, but her house was like a bug resort, and she'd grown accustomed to their presence. Yawning, she asked, "Are you the messenger?" Fairday's eyelids drooped as she turned out the lamp. Her mind floated off, and she could sense shadows creeping around the edges of her dream. The hush of sleep fell over the room, and eight hairy legs scurried off into darkness.

Two

A FRANTIC FLIGHT

Fairday hurried down her driveway. It was ten minutes before noon on Saturday, and hopefully, Lizzy was on her way. She slipped on wet leaves, and her backpack banged with a thud. A muffled whistling hiss came from inside. "Sorry!" Fairday said, adjusting the straps, then she set off down the twisting road again. The iron gates that guarded her house came into view as she turned a corner and slowed her pace.

Fairday stopped to catch her breath, inhaling the damp earthy smells. The air was crisp, but the sun was shining. Looking back at her house, she recalled Margo's words when they'd first arrived at their new home. She'd pointed a pudgy finger at the toppling, crooked manor with its peeling paint and loose shutters and proclaimed it, "Uggy."

Fairday had agreed with Margo then, but now she knew it had character. Every room probably kept a secret. Her mind stirred up the odd clues the DMS had uncovered on their last case, like the blueprints that controlled her house with rhyming riddles, and the brass key that opened the ancient mirror and caused the willow tree to attack them. Fairday's ankle twitched as she remembered the scratchy feeling when a branch tried to pull her off the third-floor balcony. Thank goodness *that* enchantment had broken. Hopefully, her recent encounter with the willow was due to wicked weather, not a curse.

A rumbling engine vibrating through the trees snapped her out of the memory. Marcus zoomed over the hill on his ATV. Fairday had met Marcus at school. Seeing the way he had beaten a bully by winning a race instead of fighting had earned him her respect. He'd been clever enough to solve the initiation riddle for the DMS (Riddle of the Sphinx), which was lucky because they couldn't have solved their last case without Marcus's awesome memory and access to stellar spy gear (his dad was in the FBI).

"Did I miss it? Is Lizzy here?" He killed the motor and took off his helmet, resting it on the handlebars. "The trail that connects our yards is a swamp pit today. It wasn't easy navigating through the muck!"

"Not yet. Should be any minute," Fairday said. "If all went as planned, that is."

"How'd she manage to sneak away? She's still coming to your Halloween party next Saturday, right?" Marcus wiped sweat from his brow, his dark skin glistening.

"Yeah, she'll be here. Luckily, Lizzy's older brother is home from college. He's in charge because her mom had plans. When she asked him if it was okay to spend the weekend at my house, he said yes right away."

"Nice. What about your parents?"

"They also said it was fine, and no one seems concerned with how she's getting here. Lizzy's brother thought we were picking her up, and my parents figured she'd be dropped off." Fairday shrugged, then pointed to a red speck speeding through the sky. "Look!"

"Wow, she's coming in really fast!" Marcus said.

Cupping her hands, Fairday yelled, "Slow down!"

Lizzy was flying toward the ground, arms flailing, a look of terror plastered across her pink face. "Get out of the way! Look out below!"

Marcus and Fairday braced to catch her. Lizzy squeezed her eyes shut as she pummeled into them.

"I can't believe I survived!" she panted.

"Why were you out of control? You made it look so easy last week," Marcus said.

"Yeah, well, it turns out when you put the pedal to the metal in these shoes, they really move. I guess I need more practice," Lizzy said, fixing her blonde curls into her cloth headband. "But that was amazing! It only took me a few minutes to get here from Manhattan. Way better than sitting in the car for an hour."

"Exactly *how* do you put the pedal to the metal in shoes?" Fairday asked.

"Well, it's weird. Everything was going as planned. When I waved goodbye, Mark was playing his video game. I put on the shoes and flew around in my room for a few minutes. It was easy, just like when I first got them from Ruby."

"So then what happened?" Marcus asked.

"I went to the top of my building and jogged to get a head start. I lifted off okay, flying into the clouds so no one would see me." Lizzy's blue eyes widened as she motioned with her hands. "I heard a plane nearby and sort of panicked. All of a sudden it was like my brain and the sneakers linked up to get me out of danger. Then I flew here"—she snapped her fingers—"just like that." Sunlight made the rubies and diamonds on the shoes cast bobbing prisms around the ground, and the two black ribbons tied to each high heel rippled in the wind.

"So you just thought about coming here, and it happened?" Fairday asked.

"Yes! Well, not just thought about it, but knew it," Lizzy explained. "The ribbons wrapped around my ankles, and I blasted off." She paused, then nudged Marcus in the arm. "*Who's* the rocket now, Brocket?"

"Finally! It's about time I had some real competition."

Fairday laughed. Only someone with magical sneakers *could* beat Marcus in a race; his speed was what gave him the nickname Brocket the Rocket.

"The second I felt out of control, I wanted to stop, but the shoes wouldn't listen to me, or my thoughts, or whatever, even though I was screaming out loud *and* in my head. I think Ruby was right, flying is just the tip of the iceberg. We don't know what other powers they have."

"It'll be awesome finding out though," Marcus said. "The sneakers didn't fit Ruby, so she couldn't use their magic. You're the only one who'll be able to find out what they can *really* do."

"Yeah, it's crazy they fit you," Fairday said. "I mean, what are the chances?"

"I know, right! The only other person who could wear them was Eldrich," Lizzy said.

"Too bad Ruby's feet are so big."

"Marcus!" Lizzy looked at him indignantly.

"What?" He raised his arms. "If she had smaller feet, like yours, she'd have put the sneakers on, then flown off to freedom like she wanted." He made a flitting gesture in the air.

Lizzy frowned at him.

"Hm. I don't think it's that simple," Fairday said. "Eldrich knew Ruby wasn't going to be able to use them when she made the trade. *Those shoes* won't work for just anyone."

"How can you know that?" Marcus asked.

"Eldrich didn't want Ruby to escape. She wanted her to stay trapped on the other side of the house, stuck in the parallel world she'd created for Thurston Begonia. Since he didn't pay his debt to her, she tricked Ruby. Eldrich even put a security system in place with the hourglass. Every time Ruby left grains of sand fell. If it had run out, she'd have died. There was *no* easy way out for her."

"So you think there's something special about Lizzy?" Marcus raised his eyebrows.

"Oh, I *know* Lizzy's special!" Fairday patted her friend's shoulder.

"Ha ha. You betcha!" Lizzy blushed.

Fairday loved that her best friend still talked like she was back home in Minnesota. When Lizzy had first

14

moved to Manhattan, kids in their class had made fun of her for saying, "You betcha." She'd shrugged it off, letting them know that she could talk however she liked. Lizzy didn't let other people ruin her fun. It was why they'd become such fast friends.

Marcus tapped his chin. "Well, you're the only person I know who can travel by foot without touching the ground, that's pretty special." Leaning back, Marcus moaned. "But ugh! I wish I could wear them!"

"That would be something to see." Lizzy giggled, wiggling a glittering high heel at him. "I wish you could too!" Suddenly, she stopped and looked around.

"What's up?' Marcus asked.

"Do you hear that?" Lizzy tilted her head to the side, listening.

Fairday jolted to attention. "Oh, right! Marcus, Lizzy, get ready." The noise grew louder as she unzipped her pack. There was a clicking sound, followed by two sharp pincers poking out of the pack. Eight long creeping legs emerged, then hopped onto the ground.

∽ Three ∽

AN UNEXPECTED MESSENGER

A giant spider burst out of Fairday's pack. Lizzy shot backward as it raced across the ground toward her. "What's happening?" she asked, her voice rising.

"Just stay still, it won't hurt you," Fairday said.

"I must really trust you," Lizzy said as the spider crawled up her jeans and hopped onto her sleeve. "Ugh! What's it going to do?" she squeaked. Her expression changed as it settled next to her ear. "Holy cow! I can understand it! It's speaking perfect English!" Lizzy paused, adding, "What's that? Oh, sorry, I mean *he*."

"He?" Marcus asked.

"He says his name is Sanir."

"Sneer?"

"Sa-nir, Marcus. Shh, wait." She held up her hand as the spider's screeching grew louder. "He's saying I'm the only one who can understand him because of the magic shoes. Someone needs our help. Sanir wants us to follow him."

"Why can't he just tell you where we need to go? It'd be way faster."

Lizzy paused, listening. "Sanir says he can't tell me; he has to show us."

"Where'd you find him, Fairday?" Marcus asked.

"He found me! A branch from the willow tree broke my bedroom window during the storm last night, and a note blew in. I moved to the parlor, but before I fell asleep, I saw a spider and asked if it was the messenger. I woke up this morning to *that spider* staring into my eyes. I flung him away, but after thinking about it, I said I was going to see the one who has the shoes. The spider came out and waved his legs at me, so I opened my pack and he climbed in. Now here we are."

"So you think it's the messenger?" Marcus asked.

Before Fairday could answer, the spider launched itself at Lizzy's head. She yelped, lurching forward. "*Do not* do that again!" she hissed through clenched teeth.

Fairday and Marcus burst out laughing. Reaching over, Fairday set Sanir on the ground. "Well, I think we should follow him. Maybe there's another person trapped on the other side of the Begonia House."

"You betcha!" Lizzy nodded.

"Definitely." Marcus picked his pack up from the back of the ATV, then swung it over his shoulders. "Sounds like we need to investigate."

Lizzy unzipped her pack, adding, "Plus the notes seem really serious. I mean, it would be terrible if it's true and words in stories disappear! Looks like we've opened another case! Hang on, I need to change my footwear." Lizzy stuffed the sneakers into her pack and slipped on a pair of stylish brown boots. "Who knows what we'll uncover? Anything's possible."

"Lead the way, Sanir," Fairday said, and the spider scurried back up the path; the three detectives followed. Fairday looked up as she passed back under the gates and read the words written over them: **Fear Not The Unexpected**. She couldn't imagine what was in store for the DMS. Lizzy had said it—anything was possible.

~e Four e~

A LIGHT IN THE DARK

The spider raced up the path, looking like a dot jetting over the ground. They picked up their pace as it disappeared into the house.

Entering the foyer, Lizzy stopped short of tripping over a paint can by the door. "Right! I forgot about the construction." She caught herself on Marcus's shoulder.

Auntie Em bounded down the grand staircase, barking and wagging her stubby tail.

"Hi, drooling sausage." Lizzy patted the sniffing head at her ankles.

Satisfied all was well, Auntie Em sneezed, then waddled into the parlor.

"Yeah, it's a complete disaster." Fairday gestured to the piles of equipment. The dusty chandelier sprinkled rainbows over the scene, giving it a colorful sense of chaos. "My bedroom's off limits till the window's fixed, so I've set up DMS headquarters in the third-floor room. The frenzy hasn't reached up there yet."

"Look!" Marcus said, pointing. "The spider's under the stairs."

"Call him Sanir, Marcus." Lizzy poked his arm.

"Seems kinda weird, but I'll try."

They walked across the black-and-white checkered floor, stepping around the scattered tools. The door under the grand staircase appeared to be ordinary, though smaller than a regular door. Fairday thought it might be a broom closet or a storage cabinet—on this side of the house, in any case.

The spider crawled under the crack, came out, and went back in. A moment later he appeared, then disappeared again.

"I think he wants us to follow him," Fairday said.

"Do you think we can all fit?" Marcus asked. "It looks pretty tight."

"In this place, who knows? There could be another house in there, or something as equally incredible." Fairday remembered the first time she'd landed on the other side of the Begonia House. They'd opened a portal through the ancient mirror on the third floor that led to a replica world stuck in time on the day of Ruby's wedding. It'd been strange seeing her house look so grand.

There were no cracked walls or webby ceilings. Things had looked cheery and bright. Except for Ruby, of course.

"Should we check the blueprints? They might show us what's in there," Lizzy asked.

"I wish we could." Fairday shook her head. "But they're locked in the wardrobe on the third floor. We might lose Sanir if we go get them."

"Okay, we'll have to take our chances today." Lizzy nodded.

Bending down, Fairday turned the knob. The door opened, but it was dark inside.

Lizzy pulled the headlamp out of her pack and strapped it on. Flipping the switch, she stuck her head in. "I can't see anything, hold on." She inched in farther. "It's cramped in here. Achoo! Blahk! I just touched something gross."

Lizzy jolted out, holding her hand up. The tips of her fingers were coated with a yellow goo. Just then, Mr. Morrow strode out of the kitchen with Fairday's little sister in tow.

"Farfey!" Margo called out to Fairday.

"Well, hello, children!" Mr. Morrow said, giving them a bow, dipping Margo in one arm. "How are we today? Plotting trouble, I see." He gestured to Lizzy's headlamp.

"You betcha!" Lizzy moved her sticky hand behind her back.

"Glad to see you've arrived safely, my dear. As always, let your imaginations soar!" His tone turned serious as he added, "Remember, Fairday, your bedroom is out of order while the window's being replaced. The repairmen are fixing it this weekend, so if you need anything from your room, let me know and I'll get it. There's still glass in the carpet, and I don't want you kids getting hurt. *Capiche?*" He raised an eyebrow.

"Sure, Dad. I understand."

"Fantabulous! See you later, kiddos." Mr. Morrow saluted them, propped Margo on his shoulders, then strode away.

Once he was out of sight, Lizzy held out her hand. "Eww! Look at this!"

"What do you think it is?" Marcus asked.

Lizzy sniffed her fingertips. "I'm not sure. It smells good, actually."

Fairday and Marcus leaned in to have a whiff.

"It does," Fairday said. "Like lemons."

Wiping her hand, Lizzy said, "Okay, let's try that again. I'll be more careful this time." She stuck her head back in. "Well, I see shelves with glass jars, some are broken. Wait! There's a hatch on the floor. That must be where Sanir wants us to go."

"Is it locked?" Marcus asked.

"I don't see a lock. Hang on."

Fairday could hear her fumbling around, when suddenly, there was a bright flash.

Lizzy jumped back, covering her eyes.

"What was that? Are you alright?" Fairday asked.

"Yeah, eh, eh," Lizzy coughed.

"Did you open the hatch?" Marcus asked.

"Yup, it's open. No clue what the light was though."

"That was so weird!" Fairday said.

"It could've been a short in a fuse. Did you see a circuit breaker?" Marcus asked.

"No. There's just a step that's visible. The light came from inside."

"Where do you think it goes?" Fairday bit her lip.

"Maybe it goes to the basement," Marcus said.

"The door to the basement is right there." Fairday pointed across the hall.

"This could be another way down."

"I guess we should check," Fairday said.

Marcus and Lizzy nodded.

The detectives secured their backpacks, then turned to face the door. Lizzy led the way and Fairday and Marcus followed her in. As Lizzy stepped down, the light burst again. Fairday heard a shriek and watched her friend tumble into darkness.

"Lizzy!" Fairday yelled, jumping in. For an instant she was blinded, and then she fell. Even though she was screaming, she couldn't hear her voice. Feeling her backpack shift and begin sliding off, Fairday made a grab for it, but it vanished. Out of the corner of her eye, she saw the flash and knew Marcus had taken the plunge too.

~ Five ~

DOWN THE HATCH

Fairday floated down through darkness. Choking back fear, she stretched out her arms and tried to relax. It felt like forever since she'd jumped into the hatch. Where were Marcus and Lizzy? Were they still falling too?

Tiny lights illuminated the space. They zipped around, encircling Fairday's body. She reached out to catch one, but there was nothing there. Suddenly, a window appeared to her right, hovering just out of reach. Fairday could see a vase with red roses behind fluttering curtains. A silver spoon on the sill caught her eye, but before she could get a better look, the window disappeared.

The circling lights followed her down, bringing a second window into view. This one was blocked by thick blinds. Even stranger, Fairday could now hear a ticking clock.

She closed her eyes and tried to calm down. Maybe this was a dream. Maybe she'd wake up in bed and everything would be fine. Pinching herself, Fairday opened her eyes, but the scene hadn't changed. This was definitely not a dream! *Tick tock. Tick tock. Tick tock.* The sound echoed and the dizzying lights flickered.

A third window came into view. It had no curtains or blinds, just colored jars on the sill behind broken glass. They reminded her of the ones under the stairs. This time, she gathered all her strength and attempted to grab the windowsill. Fairday flapped her arms, performing an erratic form of doggy paddle, trying to propel herself up. No such luck. All she could do was watch the window pass by. The lights began to disperse, leaving Fairday in the dark again. She couldn't help feeling like Alice in Wonderland, but what waited for her at the bottom of *this* rabbit hole?

Fairday felt like she was separating from her body. There was no pain, but the sensation terrified her. Feeling faint, she struggled to stay aware. Another flash exploded, and in that instant, a spiraling black hole opened below her feet.

Panic swept over her as she pumped her arms and legs as hard as she could. But it made no difference. Even if she could stop herself from entering the vortex, she'd never make it back up to the hatch. Fairday ceased struggling and let go. She squeezed her eyes shut and spun into the unknown.

"Fairday! Thank goodness you're okay."

Fairday opened her eyes to find Lizzy grasping her shoulders. *What a relief!* They were on a dock, but instead of being surrounded by water, it was listing in emptiness. A hanging lantern lit up a red door with no knob and nothing around it. A door to nowhere? *Things just kept getting stranger!*

"Did Marcus make it?" Fairday asked, her legs feeling like jelly.

"He's not here."

"I know he jumped. I saw the light."

Just as the words left her mouth, they heard a whooping yell. Marcus came flying at them, feet ready to land. "BOOM! I'm here," he announced, touching down with authority.

Fairday couldn't help but be impressed—she'd practically fainted on her trip.

"Looks like you had a blast, Brocket." Lizzy smirked.

"That's my style."

"Did you guys see the three windows?" Fairday asked.

"You betcha! I wonder what they mean?"

Fairday shrugged and looked around. Pointing at the door, she shouted, "Our packs!"

"They weren't there a second ago," Lizzy said.

As the kids moved to get their stuff, a note slid out from under the door. Fairday froze. Could it be another message from Sanir? Or was someone else behind the red door?

~e Six e~

THE KEY TO NOWHERE

Fairday bent down and picked up the note. With a glance at her partners, she read aloud: *When alas you're in Nowhere, keep your wits and be aware. Stories live behind this door, kept in time forevermore. Three windows pass, each a clue. Wordcasters know what to do. Solve the riddle to enter the Talking Library.*

Taking a deep breath, she read on:

> **Ruby's reds lift blues. Silver's found in shoes. Clock's ticking, not for long. Blinds rise, forget the song. Right colors mixed well have a potent purple smell. Feed a spoonful to your head. Sing the password you've been fed.**

"Another rhyming riddle!" Lizzy exclaimed, bouncing on tiptoes. "Good thing you're an expert when it comes to anything word related, Fairday."

Normally, Fairday would have felt proud at her friend's compliment, but her stomach was full of hornets, and her brain couldn't focus. She needed to calm down.

"So this is Nowhere," Marcus said.

"Yeah, looks like it," Fairday agreed. "I wonder what the Talking Library is?"

"It must be where we're supposed to go. I mean, that's where a librarian would be," Lizzy said. "Read it again, only slower this time."

Fairday read, "'Three windows pass, each a clue. Wordcasters know what to do.' So, the windows are clues, but what's a Wordcaster?"

"No idea. But it'd be great if one were here now," Marcus said.

"Maybe a Wordcaster is someone who catches onto words," Lizzy suggested.

"What do you mean?"

"Well, it makes me think of a fisherman casting his net. Maybe a Wordcaster casts lines to catch words. They'd be someone like you, Fairday. With your way with words, you'd be a gold medalist at the sport of Wordcasting, for sure," Lizzy said.

"Wordcasting?" Fairday raised an eyebrow.

"You betcha! If we played that in gym, it'd be your favorite subject. You'd be like, rhyme's off! You're out!" Lizzy said, pointing dramatically at Marcus.

"It wouldn't be considered a sport," Marcus said. "Not very athletic."

"Well, maybe you'd have to dribble a ball at the same time." Lizzy smirked. She turned to Fairday and added, "So, *Wordcaster*, what do you think?"

"Well, 'Ruby's reds lift blues' must be a reference to Ruby's favorite flowers, which we know from our last case are roses. 'Silver's found in shoes' may be directions to use the high-heeled sneakers to get the silver spoon. But we'd need to fly back through the vortex."

"*That* should be interesting," Lizzy muttered.

"Then, it says, 'Clock's ticking, not for long. Blinds rise, forget the song.' So I think that means if the blinds open all the way, time's up. The song could be a reference to the password."

"I wonder what's behind the blinds?" Lizzy asked.

"Let's hope we don't have to find out." Marcus rubbed the back of his neck.

Fairday read on, "Okay, here's the tricky part: 'Right colors mixed well have a potent purple smell. Feed a spoonful to your head. Sing the password you've been fed.' This could mean that we need to get a jar from the third window and take a spoonful of whatever's in it; according to this riddle, it should smell purple. What's purple smell like?"

"Grape maybe?" Lizzy scrunched up her nose.

"The jars weren't purple. They were red, blue, and yellow. Primary colors," Marcus said.

Fairday couldn't recall the colors in the jars, but she remembered the lemony goo on Lizzy's fingers. An idea popped into her head. "Hey! Maybe we have to make a purple elixir?"

"That makes sense! Red and blue make purple." Marcus snapped his fingers.

"So we need to get the silver spoon and mix together the blue and red liquid. If the potion smells like grape, we'll each take a spoonful. If we do it in time, we'll sing a song that opens the Talking Library." Just as Fairday finished, a ticking clock broke the stillness.

"I think we'd better get going," Marcus said.

Lizzy whipped out the sneakers from her pack. "Fairday, hop onto my back. You'll need to grab what we need from the windows, and I'll do my best to keep us steady. Hopefully, the sneakers will do what I think they will. But you'd better hang on tight."

"Wait. What?"

"It's fine, Fairday! Get on! Marcus, think purple thoughts."

"This is crazy," Marcus said. "Be careful, fly fast!"

Feeling both scared and determined, Fairday jumped onto Lizzy's back and held on tight. Lizzy bent her knees to get in position. Fairday looked down just in time to see the black ribbons wrap around Lizzy's ankles before they took off.

Fairday focused on what needed to be done. Hang on, get the spoon, get the two jars. Was their plan going to work? Every bone in her body wished the answer to that question was yes. Squeezing her eyes shut, they blasted through the center of the black hole.

~ Seven ~
A COLLECTION OF CLUES

A rush of air hit Fairday's face as they sped out of the vortex. She willed her eyes open, even though it felt safer to keep them closed. The ticking echoed all around as they rocketed up.

Specks of lights appeared, and Fairday saw the window with the roses.

"I'm going to hover, so you can grab the spoon," Lizzy yelled.

"What's happening? You missed it!" Fairday shouted as they flew past it into emptiness.

"Shh. No talking. I'm concentrating." Lizzy slammed on the brakes. Jerkily, she lowered them to the sill. "That's as close as I can get."

Fairday reached for the spoon, but they swerved. "Rats! I missed."

"Shift to the right." Lizzy shot up again.

Pass two. They careened sideways. "Almost had it!" Fairday said.

Lizzy moaned and got back on track.

Fairday stretched as far as she could and caught the handle with her fingertips. "Got it!" She stuck the spoon in her back pocket.

Lizzy punched the air. "Yes! I knew we could do it!"

"What happens now?"

"The vortex will pull us down to the window with the jars."

"The window's broken on that one, it's gonna be tricky."

Lizzy nodded and the two girls fell, rippling through space. The lights circled them, like fireflies in the dark. The ticking was a constant reminder that time was running out.

As the window with the blinds came into view, Fairday noticed they'd opened more than halfway. Had they wasted too much time? She focused and saw figures moving behind the slats.

"Lizzy, are you seeing what I'm seeing?"

"Yep—people walking around in circles. They remind me of the ghosts we saw on the other side of the Begonia House. Too bad we don't have Marcus's infrared goggles, then we could confirm if they're alive or not. That's how we were able to tell in the last case."

"*Those* ghosts seemed happy," Fairday said. The shadowy guests at Ruby's wedding were having a grand time at the party, and didn't pay them any mind. These figures had a grim feeling about them, and their circular pace gave her the creeps. Fairday didn't know why the scene disturbed her so much, but it did. Without warning, a giant eye opened behind the blinds. In a blink it was gone, but she'd seen fire in its gaze, and fear struck her heart. "Oh!" she yelled.

"What happened?"

"Did you see *that*?"

"What?"

"That big eye! It looked right at us!"

"I didn't see an eye." Pointing, Lizzy shouted, "Here comes the next window!"

Fairday's hands shook. The eye had terrified her, but she needed to focus. *Hold on, don't lose the spoon, get the blue and red jars.* Fairday set the thoughts on a loop in her head.

"Here we go," Lizzy shouted.

Positioning herself on Lizzy's shoulders, Fairday leaned out.

As the window came into view, Lizzy steered close. Fairday could see perfectly. The glass was cracked and there was an opening where she could reach in, but one wrong move and she'd slice her arm. "I can get them, but I might get cut."

"It's too dangerous. I'm not very good at hovering yet," Lizzy said.

"What should we do?"

"Break the glass with the spoon."

"What if I drop it?"

"We'll have to take that chance!"

Fairday took the spoon out of her pocket and hit the glass. Shards flew off and one caught her hand. "Ouch!"

"Are you okay?"

"Glass cut my hand! I'm alright though." Blood trickled through Fairday's fingers and the spoon slipped. "Oh no! I dropped it!"

"Don't worry! Just get the jars."

Fairday ignored the pain and grabbed the blue one, handing it down to Lizzy. As soon as she had the red jar, alarm bells blared.

"Hold on!" Lizzy yelled. "Let's get back to the dock."

Fairday gripped the red jar with her good hand as they flew down into the swirling air. Her mind was reeling as she clung to Lizzy. Would they make it back in time? Was it possible to complete the challenge without the spoon?

～ Eight ～

VANISHING FROM NOWHERE

As they blasted out of the vortex and headed for the dock, Fairday could see Marcus waving his arms below. The alarm bells fell silent when they approached the platform. Once the landing was close enough, Fairday leaped off Lizzy's back. *Thud.* They were there. Relief washed over her.

"That was a smooth landing," Lizzy said.

"Yeah, it was. Hey, Mar—"

"Are you guys trying to kill me?" Marcus waved the silver spoon at them. "This thing nearly knocked me out. If it wasn't for my catlike reflexes, I'd be toast."

"Awesome, Marcus! You found it!" Lizzy hugged him.

"Nice. I'm almost killed, and she's excited about it."

"Sorry! You know I'm glad you lived." Lizzy grinned.

"It was crazy up there!" Fairday said. "A piece of glass cut me, and I dropped the spoon." She held out a jittery hand. The wound looked painful, but it was more of a scratch than a cut.

Lizzy took off her headband and gave it to Fairday. "Here, wrap it with this."

"Thanks," Fairday said, tying it around her hand.

"The alarm went off and the blinds are almost up," Lizzy said.

"Quick, take your packs." Marcus tossed them over. "You never know when we'll need our spy gear."

The two girls gave him the jars, then swung their packs on.

"Marcus, pour some from the red jar into the blue one," Lizzy instructed, "then mix it with the spoon."

"Hurry," Fairday said, biting her thumbnail.

Marcus gave the solution a good stir. "Well, it's purple and smells grape. Bottoms up!" He gulped down a spoonful.

Lizzy didn't hesitate and took hers, then passed the spoon to Fairday.

Ugh, grape. Blahk, Fairday thought, but made herself swallow, praying it wasn't poison. Feeling like Alice again, she wondered what was going to happen. Would they shrink or grow?

The three friends watched each other in anticipation. Suddenly, they all belted out the chorus to "The Purple People Eater."

Fairday touched the corners of her mouth, shocked by the words that burst out. What a strange feeling! Just then, a buzzing vibrated around them and the scene changed.

"Look!" Fairday pointed at the red door, which began to fade. Everything was dissolving. The edges of the dock were getting foggy, and the lantern light was dimming. Fairday's friends were also starting to blur.

"This is weird!" Lizzy's voice sounded hollow.

"Lizzy! Marcus!" Fairday yelled, but only the top of Marcus's head was visible. She looked down and realized she was almost gone too!

Fairday was certain they'd solved the riddle, but shouldn't the door have opened? Trying to be brave, she vanished out of Nowhere.

~ Nine ~

THE WORDWEAVERS

The scene rematerialized around Fairday. Her friends were by her side, both unharmed. *Phew!* They'd all made it. Fairday's eyes focused on a figure in a dark cloak standing before them. In the background, she could make out gray walls. Did they wind up in a dungeon?

"You three solved the riddle in time. Well done." The stranger loomed closer. He brushed a pale wisp of hair from his face and extended a hand. "I am Fas, the Librarian."

Fairday unstuck her tongue. "I'm Fairday, and these are my friends, Marcus and Lizzy. We're the Detective Mystery Squad, and we've come to help."

"Now that you've met the challenge, the Talking Library will permit you to enter," Fas said. "And I am grateful for it. Your help *is* needed." He gestured for them to sit at a table that stretched across the room.

Fairday peered in. If this was a library, where were all the books? There were four stone walls and one door. A chandelier hung in the center, casting dim light across the wooden table. Fairday caught sight of a person sitting in a dark corner. "Who's that?" she asked.

"Ah, yes. I almost forgot. This is my son, Sanir," Fas said, beckoning him closer.

"You mean the spider?" Marcus asked.

"Marcus!" Lizzy pinched him.

"Yes," Fas answered. "My son can transform into a spider in your world."

Sanir skulked around the table. His black hair was slicked into a ponytail. He stood in front of them, twisting his fingers. "Hello."

"Hi," Fairday said. "Nice to meet you in person."

"Hey." Marcus nodded.

"Well, Sanir, I feel like we're old friends," Lizzy joked.

Sanir's eyes flicked toward Lizzy, then fell as Fas gave him a brisk pat and gently pushed him away. "You've done as I've asked. Now go."

"Yes, Father." Sanir shot them a dark glance and turned to leave.

Fairday's eyes followed him. As Sanir went through the door, a book fluttered out, then soared back in over his head before he shut it. *Was that a flying book?* Fairday could tell by Lizzy's face, she'd seen it too.

"Please, sit," Fas said.

The table had five chairs around it, each in a different style. Fairday selected one with lionhead armrests. Lizzy picked a seat with feathers, and Marcus's had arrows for legs.

Fas pulled out a chair with webbing on it. Before sitting, he glanced around the table and said, "I'm glad to see we all know who we are." He shifted into the seat and rested his fingers over the onyx spiders at the ends of the armrests.

"Whadda you mean?" Marcus asked.

He gave him a thin smile. "It is a marvelous skill to recognize who you are, and who you are not. I can tell when I'm in good company." His violet eyes fell on each of them in turn.

Marcus raised his eyebrows. Lizzy's expression was blank.

"Is this the Talking Library?" Fairday asked. *The DMS needed some answers!*

"The library lies beyond that door." Fas pointed.

"Do you and your son live here?" Marcus asked.

"This place has been our home from the beginning."

"The beginning of what?"

"The story, of course," Fas said.

"Which one?" Lizzy chimed in.

"That's the question, isn't it?" Leaning back, he entwined his fingers. "Sanir and I are Wordweavers, storykeepers like

44

the great Anansi. The Talking Library holds the collected tales of humankind, and we are its guardians."

"What *is* a Talking Library?" Fairday spoke up.

Fas fixed his eyes on her. "It's where books live out their storylines."

"Huh?" Marcus said and leaned forward, arms crossed on the table.

"I'll try to explain." Fas rubbed his temple. "When stories are conceived by creators, such as yourselves, ideas flood the mind and gather in pools."

"By us, you mean, human beings?" Marcus asked.

"Yes, humans are creators, and they're powerful, though most doubt their own abilities." Fas pushed back his chair and stood up. He began to pace. "Thought ink spills into the deep well of the living mind. When you dip into it, words form and sink into empty spaces." He paused to look at them. "It's very exciting when that happens. This chandelier glows blue to alert me when a new story is being born." Fas gestured overhead.

"What's thought ink?" Lizzy asked, glancing up.

"It's light that sees dark," Fas answered.

"I'm sorry, I don't understand. How does light *see* dark?" Fairday looked at Lizzy and Marcus, they seemed confused too.

45

Fas scratched his chin. "I suppose it's similar to a black hole in space." He paused, then made an arch in the air with his finger. "Bent light is the main ingredient in thought ink."

"Light can't escape black holes. That's why they're like a void," Marcus said and leaned back in his chair.

Fas raised his hands. "Light spiraling into a black hole gives emptiness form, like how sentences bring out images in the mind's eye. You don't see a picture when you read a book, only words in lines. Their meaning is defined by how they fall on the page. When the scenes come to life, that's storymagic. Possibilities are endless, and the library continues to expand."

"But why is it called the *Talking* Library?" Lizzy asked.

"Books are free to be themselves here. If one chooses to do so, it may talk to you."

Fairday raised an eyebrow. "You mean you can chat with a book?" If that was true, she could hardly contain herself. The chance to discuss characters she loved with the actual books! How cool was that? She had to stop her mind from starting a list of the ones she wanted to have at a reading club. Lizzy was wide eyed, staring at Fas.

"Yes. You can talk to the books, the characters, the narrators, even visit the scenes by smelling the pages." The corners of Fas's mouth turned up; clearly, he could sense their delight. "Sanir and I are here to keep their stories straight, and we've been doing it for ages, but now a bookworm has been set loose in the library, and words are being devoured. If the original story is changed, then copies of the books in your world are altered as well."

"How does *that* work?" Marcus asked.

"Books bound in your world are destroyed by time or human carelessness. Up until now, neither has had any influence here, and storylines can play out forever."

"So this is where the real first edition of every book is?" Marcus raised his eyebrows.

"Yes. Every book in existence is copied from our collection." Fas tapped a long finger on the table. The chandelier flickered above them.

"And now a bookworm's eating their words?"

"Exactly. It's changing stories and destroying the books' lives."

Fairday remembered the passage from *The Wizard of Oz* that'd been missing words. Could a bookworm really be eating them? Fas said he and Sanir were like Anansi, and Fairday knew from her own love of reading that Anansi was a deity who used words to get his way. What if Fas was trying to trick them?

"How do we know you're telling the truth?" Fairday asked, excited by the idea of making friends with books, but wary of the situation.

"You can't," Fas said, eyes alight. "Come with me, and we'll see if what I say sticks." His cloak fanned out as he swept across the room. The door opened at a touch of his finger. Turning, he said, "Welcome to the Talking Library."

~ Ten ~

THE TALKING LIBRARY

There were books everywhere! Bookshelves circled the entire room, creating hallways that faded off around corners. Fairday's eyes grew wide. Rolling shelf ladders were positioned at various levels, begging her to climb aboard and start searching the stacks. In the center, there was a stone hearth that rose up, with no ceiling in sight. Statues carved as guards stood on either side of the mantel, swords crossed over the flames. A plush red couch and an antique writing desk were set upon a decorative carpet, similar to the lion-and-unicorn rug in Fairday's bedroom.

Fas motioned for them to sit on the couch.

"Pinch me," Lizzy whispered to Fairday.

"I know, right!" She breathed in the book smell. *Had she found heaven?*

"Wow, this place is enormous!" Marcus exclaimed.

"It's no size at all, given the fact that it doesn't exist." Fas sat at the desk. He pushed aside a few books, which shuddered and shook, pages flapping.

"How can it not exist? I can see it," Marcus said.

"Nothing you see is real, my boy. You'll learn that soon enough," Fas said. In a gentler voice, he added, "I'm thankful you've come."

"Why do you need our help?" Fairday asked.

"The situation is dire. Something like this has never happened, and I'm afraid I don't have the answers." Fas closed his eyes, shaking his head. "I never thought it would come to this, but there is no other way to stop the bookworm. I must reach the Myxtress, Eldrich."

"Do you mean *Mistress*?" Marcus scratched his head. "I thought Eldrich was a gypsy."

"No, Eldrich is not a gypsy. That is a misused human term used to hurt a certain group of people. Her proper title is Myxtress, spelled with a *y*, *x*— and her nature is as mysterious as that of the letter *y*."

"Huh?" Lizzy tilted her head.

"*Y* presents itself as both a vowel and a consonant, according to where it appears in a word. A Myxtress possesses the power to shift character roles. Similar to a Wordweaver, such as myself, they play a hand in the creation of storymagic. But unlike me, Eldrich answers to nobody and isn't subject to following rules. Her magic deals in mixed meanings, and it's impossible to understand without eons of study." Fas looked at them, violet eyes flashing.

"If you know Eldrich, then why can't you contact her?" Marcus asked.

"The ancient council I report to forbids me from summoning her regarding this matter." Fas leaned forward. "I need *you three* to bring her here, and I can't tell you anymore than that. I've already said too much."

"How are we supposed to contact her?" Marcus glanced at Lizzy and Fairday.

Fairday remembered a clue from their last case and raised her hand. "I think I know. Thurston Begonia mentioned in a letter we found that Eldrich sold him a blue glass ball, and that if he ever wanted to contact her, he could hold it and call her name. Then she'd appear."

"Right! Good thinking! He used it to reach her, and that's how the magic blueprints for the Begonia House came to be." Lizzy beamed at Fairday.

"You guys, remember, I, uh, sort of broke something that fits that description, right?" Marcus said sheepishly.

"That's true," Lizzy said.

"Maybe that was just a knickknack," Fairday said, remembering the sound *that* glass ball had made when it crashed to the floor during their last investigation.

"Possibly, or we might be able to use the sneakers somehow. I just don't know what we'd have to do." Lizzy tapped her chin.

"Let's hope you can figure it out," Fas said. "I can tell you that the only person who may know how to contact Eldrich is Ruby. But I must warn you, Ruby doesn't know anything about Sanir and me, nor the Talking Library, for that matter."

"How can she *not* know about all this?" Fairday asked, gesturing to the endless hallways of books. Ruby had been trapped in the Begonia House for so long, she *must* have opened the hatch under the stairs. The house's magic had become part of her. How could she have missed the portal to the Talking Library?

"It's not our place to interfere with the Housekeeper. Access to the library was not granted to Ruby, so the portal in the hatch wasn't there. Normally, it opens to a root cellar."

"What do you mean, Housekeeper? I don't think Ruby cleaned much," Marcus said.

"A Housekeeper is a person who lives in a memory and is linked to the Talking Library. As the Librarian, one of my responsibilities is to siphon thought ink from the storypools in their imagination. Library rules are written with it, and I *do not* know what will happen when the ink runs out. It will be chaos if I can't keep storylines in order. The books will fall to pieces here, as they will in your world."

"Does it hurt when you collect the thought ink?" Lizzy scrunched up her nose.

Fas smiled. "No, it doesn't hurt, child. Here, let me show you." He picked up a feather quill from the desk and dipped it into a crystal inkwell. A blank sheet of paper appeared before him, and he dotted the center of it. "Now, watch."

The three kids leaned in. Ink pooled in the middle of the dot before seeping into the page. Fairday looked closer and gasped. She could see an eye inside the black bubble! It blinked, then broke into swirling lines. As they spread out like veins onto the page, the image of the fiery eye she'd seen behind the blinds caused a chill to touch her spine.

"Thought ink is alive." Fas pointed to the crystal inkwell. "And this inkwell is enchanted by ancient magic that tethers the Housekeeper's mind to the Talking Library. The one connected isn't harmed, or even aware it's happening, but they must agree to live in a memory."

"But Ruby was tricked by Eldrich," Fairday said. On their last case, Ruby described how Eldrich had appeared on her wedding day as an old scruffy woman and offered her a trade. Ruby agreed to swap her natural charms for the magic high-heeled sneakers. When the shoes didn't fit, Eldrich turned into a beautiful woman, and Ruby became a hag. Instead of facing the world as a monster, Ruby chose to go through the mirror and live in the memory of her wedding day, where she'd remain like she was before the deal, but she could never leave.

"Unfortunately for Ruby, it didn't matter. It was under unusual circumstances she became involved, but she filled the role as Housekeeper and the thought ink continued to flow. When Eldrich's curse broke and Ruby left the Begonia House, access to the living mind was shut off. Ink supplies are low, and the library has become"—he paused—"vulnerable." He gestured to the crystal inkwell. It was less than half full.

"So you want us to ask Ruby if she knows how to find Eldrich?"

"Yes."

"Well, we know where Ruby is, so that's not a problem," Lizzy said. "But I can't imagine she'd want to see Eldrich again. Why would she help us?"

"The fate of all the stories that ever were or ever will be depends on your success, so you must do whatever's needed. As Librarian of the Talking Library, it's my aim to keep storylines straight, but only a Myxtress can cast the right words to bind a bookworm." Fas walked over to the hearth and stared at the flames. His silver hair lit up as he turned to them. "Beware of Eldrich—she's an ancient and clever being, neither good nor bad, and she dwells in and out of time. Her nature isn't evil, but she'll only offer something in return for gain."

"Even if we find Eldrich, how're we supposed to get her here?" Marcus asked.

"Cross that bridge when you come to it. I imagine an opportunity will present itself."

"Will we need to jump down the hatch?" Lizzy asked.

"No, there are other ways to access the portal, which will become known to you soon. You three have proven yourselves worthy. Besides, you're accompanied by a Wordcaster." Fas turned to Fairday. "It's a rare treat for me to make your acquaintance."

"I knew it!" Lizzy grinned, nudging Fairday.

"Thanks. I'm not sure what that means, but I have an idea." Fairday blushed.

A smile crept onto Fas's lips. "It is a unique person who has an intimate connection to words. So few understand them or are able to turn them around using their senses. You *feel* words, and that gift will come in handy as you begin your work."

A book fluttered in front of Fas. He reached out and grabbed it, snapping it shut. "You figured out how to enter the Talking Library, and I have no doubt you'll figure out how to get back. When the time comes, believe in yourselves, and the right path will present itself." He opened his arms to them. "The library is yours to use for now. I bid you good luck and goodbye." Fas placed the book down on the desk, then turned to go. His cloak trailed behind as he disappeared through the door, leaving the DMS to find their way home.

~ Eleven ~
USEFUL, HARMFUL, INTERESTING?

"As much as I feel like I just got my invitation to Hogwarts, I'm a little concerned about getting back," Fairday said, her eyes following a book whizzing by. Turning to face her friends, she added, "I mean, look at the size of this place. There are so many books!"

"Plus we might have to catch them first," Lizzy said.

"Or smell them." Marcus stood up and walked over to the desk. Picking up the one that Fas had set down, he said, "Maybe this'll help?"

"What is it?" Lizzy asked.

"Its title is USEFUL."

"Excellent! That sounds like a good place to start." Fairday hurried over.

The book had a white title and a black cover. There were no other markings or inscriptions. Fairday tried to open it, but the binding wouldn't budge. "It won't open."

"Whadda you mean?" Lizzy asked. She tried it too, but no such luck. Shrugging, she gave the book back to Fairday.

"Weird," Fairday said, turning it over in her hands. "I guess it's not so useful after all. I wish I knew what to do."

"Be nice," a strange voice said through her fingers.

"Oh!" Fairday jumped back.

"Who said that?" Marcus asked.

"The book!" Fairday held it up. A mouth had split open underneath the title and two blinking eyes popped out of the cover.

"Maybe this is like the furniture in the Begonia House, and you have to ask it politely," Marcus suggested, staring at the odd face.

Fairday recalled how Marcus had remembered the riddle from the blueprints and asked the wardrobe to help them capture Ruby. It didn't work until he remembered to say please.

"Alright. Hello. Would you *please* tell us how to get home?"

The book grinned, showing teeth made of pages. "Of course! I'm USEFUL." It beamed, but the smile vanished as another book fell from above, knocking it out of Fairday's hand.

"Liar!" it bellowed, landing on the desk. "Liar and a sham. Trickery! I say, trickery!"

"Stay out of this, you soggy binding of dribble drabble. Get back to the shelf where you belong." USEFUL flapped up to the desk. "Excuse the *rude* interruption. Fas wanted you to find me and you have. Very clever."

"Don't listen to him, I say!" the other book pleaded. It was yellow with a jagged mouth and shifting eyes.

"Well, *who* are you?" Fairday asked.

The title flashed at them, which read **HARMFUL** in black letters. At that moment, a third book materialized on the desk.

HARMFUL bristled. "Oh, it's only *Interesting*," he said, ruffling his pages.

This one was red with a silver title. Feline eyes were fixed in a blank stare, and its lopsided smile reminded Fairday of the Cheshire Cat. The book's eyes spun around, its grin widening, like it had heard her thoughts.

"I think she likes you." USEFUL winked at Fairday.

"So are you three like a set of guide books?" Lizzy asked.

"Correct," USEFUL said.

"NOT!" **HARMFUL** yelled.

Interesting blinked.

"Who should we believe?" Marcus asked.

Lizzy squared her shoulders. "Listen, books, can you help us or not?"

"Yes!" USEFUL exclaimed.

"No!" **HARMFUL** declared.

Interesting fell over.

"Why shouldn't we trust a book that's called USEFUL?" Fairday asked.

"I can't tell you," **HARMFUL** said, biting his lip. "It's a secret, and I have to stay with my set. But be warned, I say!"

"He thinks everything's a conspiracy. If I wasn't bound to him by Fas, he'd be in the trash bin by now." USEFUL glared at **HARMFUL**.

"What about *Interesting*?" Fairday asked.

"Why, she's quite mad, of course." USEFUL's eyes shifted toward the red book tottering in circles. Suddenly, *Interesting* tipped off the desk. Fairday leaped to catch the book, but it rematerialized in her hands, eyes spinning, mouth grinning, cover *purring?* She loved the crazy cat face and gave the spine a pat before setting it down.

"Let's just ask and see what happens," Marcus said.

Fairday shrugged. "Can *one* of you please tell us how to get back to the Begonia House?"

"Of course!" USEFUL said and plopped flat on the desk, pages flipping. When they stopped, he continued, "Written here is the answer you seek."

HARMFUL ruffled, but remained silent. *Interesting* let out a deep snore.

Fairday leaned over the book. "I don't believe it, another riddle." Flexing her fingers, she read aloud:

> **"To get back to where you were before, you must seek out the common door. Move ahead, a queen's delight; pass her by when the heart's set right. Looking through, the reflection's clear; what you see isn't here. When in doubt, ask a book, but beware the Shadow Rook."**

Fairday picked up USEFUL, turning it over. "Hey! The face is gone."

"The others have disappeared too! I guess they're not the books we're supposed to ask," Lizzy said. "I wonder what a Shadow Rook is?"

"A rook's a chess piece, it's also called a castle. Plus I think they're birds, like crows. I've never heard of a 'Shadow' Rook though," Marcus said.

"It doesn't sound like a good thing," Lizzy said.

Marcus nodded. "So we need to find a door?"

"The riddle also mentions a reflection, which points to a mirror," Fairday said.

"Could it be talking about the ancient mirror on the third floor? We know the door that appears in that one is a portal to the other side of the Begonia House," Lizzy suggested.

"Maybe. Wait, there's something scribbled at the bottom." Fairday held the page closer. "It says, 'Go ask Alice.'"

Lizzy leaned in. "The writing's smudged, like it's been erased. That's suspicious," she said. "We don't know who wrote this. It could be misleading."

"Yeah, but Fas *wants* us to solve this mystery. I think he wrote the clue because he couldn't mention it himself," Marcus said.

"Possibly," Lizzy said. "Hmm—go ask Alice. I feel like that's a song my Aunt Forsey likes to sing. This must be about *Alice in Wonderland*, right?"

"Yeah, for sure," Fairday said. "The whole case is like falling down the rabbit hole, plus it makes sense with the riddle. I'm guessing we need to find Alice, then ask her about a mirror."

"I wonder how we summon her?" Lizzy asked.

At that moment the walls shook, shelf ladders rattled, and books fell to the floor. "What's happening?" Fairday braced herself on the desk.

"I don't know!" Lizzy grabbed onto Marcus.

"It's an earthquake!" Marcus yelled.

"I don't think we're on Earth, Marcus," Lizzy shot back.

All at once, everything became very still, then a rumbling vibration gripped Fairday. When it ceased, a book fell from above and landed at her feet. Its cover was ripped, like it had been clawed. Fairday bent down and picked it up. "Oh my gosh! Look at this." The binding fell apart as the pages from *Alice in Wonderland* dropped to the floor.

~ Twelve ~
ALICE'S ANSWER

"Now what do we do?" Fairday held up what was left of the book.

"I won't!" a panicked voice shouted from the pages on the floor.

"Who's that?" Marcus jumped.

Lizzy bent down and asked, "Is someone there?"

"I can't," the voice cried.

"It's okay, we're not going to hurt you," Lizzy soothed. "Can you come out?"

"Ye—yes," the book sobbed, then began to twitch. All at once its pages swirled up into a paper girl with words flowing around her like living sentences.

"What's wrong?" Fairday asked.

"I—I can't say," she choked out, her head in her hands.

"Are you Alice?"

"Ye—yes."

"Can you tell us what happened to you?" Lizzy asked.

"We—well, I was ha—having tea with the Ha—Hatter when everything st—started shaking, and th—this one-eyed mo—monster swooped in and ya—yanked me from my ch—chair." She caught her breath between inky tears.

"Go on." Lizzy reached out a consoling hand.

Alice recoiled. "Don't touch me!" She glared at Lizzy; her eyes shone liquid black.

"Oh! I'm so sorry," Lizzy apologized.

"I'll bleed to death, then you'll be *sorry*."

"How will you bleed? You don't have any blood," Marcus said.

"Never *you* mind, sir. None of *your* business anyway."
Alice crossed her arms in front of her crinkled dress.

"No worries, we're not going to touch you." Fairday
picked up USEFUL from the desk. "According to this
book, you know something about a mirror that can help
us get back to the Begonia House. Is this true?"

Alice began bawling again and turned her back to
them. "Ye—yes."

"Can you tell us what to do?" Marcus asked.

"Not *you*!" Alice spun around. "I don't even like you."

"Okay, she really hates me." Marcus shrugged.

"Can you tell *me*?" Lizzy asked gently.

"No." Alice covered her mouth and giggled. "You're
too silly."

Lizzy and Marcus stared at Fairday.

"Oh, right. How about me?" Fairday gave the paper
girl a smile.

"Well." Alice considered Fairday. "I guess. But I
can't tell you the right way, only *a* way. I'll whisper, so
they won't hear."

The pages that made up Alice flew into the air. They
whirled up over Fairday like a tornado. Alice's voice
echoed in Fairday's head: *"The very first thing she did
was to look whether there was a fire in the fireplace, and*

she was quite pleased to find that there was a real one,
blazing away as brightly as the one she had left behind."
The pages fell silent, then dropped to the floor.

"Alice?" Fairday asked the pile. "Are you in there?"

"She's gone," Lizzy said.

"Thankfully." Marcus rolled his eyes.

"What'd Alice say?" Lizzy asked.

"It was about a fire, one that's real—" Fairday's words
trailed off as she walked toward the hearth. There was no
heat coming from the flames; the logs shifted and sparked,
but there was no sound. *Shouldn't it crackle?* "That's it!"

"What?" Marcus and Lizzy said in unison.

"The fire! That was Alice's clue." Fairday knelt down.

"What're you doing?" Marcus asked.

"Watch." Fairday reached her arm into the flames.

"Fairday, don't!" Lizzy rushed over.

Fairday's fingertips skimmed a cool, smooth surface.
Looking up at her friends, she said, "This fire isn't real,
it's a reflection."

~ Thirteen ~

THE SHADOW ROOK

"Oh my gosh, I never would've guessed!" Lizzy leaned into the fireplace for a better look. "It's weird that it doesn't reflect this room."

Marcus bent under the crossed swords and touched the mirror. "I wonder how this works? It must be reflecting the fire from someplace. Remember in the last case we had to use the brass key to open the mirror. Maybe there's a clue here." He stood up and started tapping the hearth.

Fairday pulled up the couch cushions and Lizzy shuffled through the desk.

"Hey! I found something," Marcus shouted from behind the fireplace.

"That was fast!" Lizzy said, and the two girls hurried to his side.

The backside of the hearth had enormous chess pieces carved into the stone. The queen was in the center, eye level with Fairday. She held a scepter that was missing its top. The king stood by her side, his crown barely reaching her shoulder. He had a dazzling heart-shaped ruby in his outstretched hands. The figures on either side of them were positioned in order of rank: bishops in sweeping robes, knights on rearing steeds, and castle towers at each end.

"Look at that ruby!" Lizzy exclaimed. "It's as big as a robin's egg! What did the riddle say about it?"

"The line was, 'Move ahead, a queen's delight; pass her by when the heart's set right,'" Marcus recited.

"Nice, Brocket! That great memory of yours comes in handy. The jewel must go in the scepter," Fairday said.

Lizzy's fingers reached out to grab the ruby. The king's hands clenched in a fist as the statue trembled, then withdrew and disappeared into a hole that opened in the hearth. The piece that looked like a castle tower rumbled out in the king's place and the stones closed behind it.

"That's the rook," Marcus said, grimly.

Fairday could see the gem sparkling through open slits at the top of the tower. It looked like a miniature fortress holding the heart.

"The holes are too narrow to reach through," Marcus said.

"Hold on," Lizzy said. "I have an idea." She rushed to the other side, then returned with their packs. "It's a long shot, but maybe we can get it with these." She dug her mom's discarded makeup tweezers out of the pocket.

"That's a great idea! But those may not be long enough." Fairday pulled the pen out of her own pack and handed it over. "This will help, you can roll it closer."

"You think you can pick up *that* gem with tweezers?" Marcus asked.

"I have many skills, Marcus Brocket, and collecting sparkly things is one of them."

"Looks like you know what you're doing," Marcus said, watching Lizzy.

"You betcha. The ruby's in the center, so I can move it over and lift it with the pen, then try to pull it out with the tweezers." Finagling the ruby, Lizzy was all business. "I'll just nudge it up the side. Almost. Okay, I've got it."

Lizzy clamped onto the jewel, but the stone slipped. "Oh no! I'm losing it!" In a panic, she dropped the tweezers and stuck her finger through the hole, trying to catch it. "OUCH!"

"What happened?" Marcus asked.

"Something bit me!" Lizzy held up her finger, which had two red dots on the tip. Dark lines began spreading fast over her hand like a web. She pushed up her shirt sleeve, panicking. "What's happening?"

"I don't know!" Fairday felt helpless as the lines snaked up Lizzy's arm.

"Does it hurt?" Marcus's faced paled.

"No! But I'm starting to fe—feel very strange," Lizzy said, collapsing to the floor.

"Lizzy!" Fairday cried and dropped to her friend's side. "What should we do?"

Marcus knelt down and shook her shoulders. "Lizzy?" No response. He turned to Fairday. "We've got to find Fas. She needs help right away."

Fairday jumped up and ran across the room to the door they came through. *Rats, no handle!* Her nerves were short-circuiting. "I don't know how to open it!" She began banging as hard as she could. "Fas, can you hear me?" There was no answer. "I don't know what to do."

A low laugh seeped around her like molasses. Turning, Fairday saw that the fire reflected in the mirror had flickered low. Darkness shifted over the winding bookcases and a bright spark lit the fireplace. Black smoke rose from the embers and spun out into the room.

"So well I find you," a raspy voice spoke as the thick cloud touched down in front of Fairday, taking the shape of a shadowy man with no face.

"I don't know who you are, but my friend is hurt and needs help." Fairday's voice shook.

"Thieves asking for help. Curious," the dark figure said.

"We're not thieves!" Fairday shouted, anger rising in her throat. "Fas invited us here and we're trying to get home. My friend was bitten by something. Can you help us or not?"

Marcus stayed quiet on the other side of the hearth and guarded Lizzy.

"Yes," it said, moving toward Fairday.

Fairday backed up an inch or so. *Maybe this wasn't such a great idea after all.*

The shadowman flickered in and out of view as it turned and glided around the hearth.

Marcus was sitting next to Lizzy; she was still unconscious. "Get back," he said.

"Your friend has asked for my help," the voice said.

"Who are you, and what are you offering?" Marcus shot back.

The riddle flashed in Fairday's mind and she blurted out, "Are you the Shadow Rook?"

"Smart girl. I am."

Had they been tricked? Lizzy had a hunch the note to ask Alice was suspicious. Alice had said she couldn't tell Fairday the right way, only a way. What did that mean? Fairday didn't know, but felt certain something had gone dreadfully wrong. *Where was Fas?*

Fourteen

POISONOUS PUNCTUATION

The Shadow Rook loomed over them. "Best if you step aside, little boy."

"I'm not little." Marcus jumped to his feet.

"If you want your friend back, you'll do as I say."

Marcus stood like a wall in front of Lizzy and looked at Fairday. They'd been warned about the Shadow Rook, but he was the only one here who could help them. Fairday's heart thudded against her chest, but she threw caution to the wind. "It's okay, Marcus. Let him by." She crossed her fingers and prayed she'd made the right decision.

"A wise move," the Shadow Rook said.

Marcus stood back, but looked ready to spring into action. Fairday was on pins and needles as she watched a dark finger reach out and touch the center of Lizzy's forehead. The inky lines on her arm retracted, then pooled in the palm of her hand. The Shadow Rook's fingers brushed over them, collecting the webby darkness like magnets attracting iron filaments.

Lizzy began to stir. She shook her head and pulled herself up. "What happened?"

"Pricked by the punctuation," the Shadow Rook answered.

"Punctuation? You mean, like a comma?" Marcus asked.

"All parts of a story work for their master," he replied, adding coyly, "if the master knows the parts of a story, that is."

As if on cue, hundreds of insect-like specks emerged from the shadows. One crept by Fairday, a black dot with eight legs propelling it forward, like a daddy longlegs. *Is that a period?* She caught sight of a semicolon scooching inch by inch up the queen's stony sleeve. Others scuttled away, and her eyes followed them.

"I didn't know punctuation could be so scary." Lizzy ducked as a question mark zoomed past her head and landed on top of the castle tower like a dragonfly. "Do they all bite?"

"Be aware, girl. When understood, everything has its price and poison," the Shadow Rook said. "Now, to settle your debt—"

"Wait. What?" Marcus interrupted.

A sinking feeling came over Fairday. "You didn't say we'd owe anything for your help."

"You didn't ask the cost," he hissed like a snake.

"You should've said there was a price!" Marcus balled his fists.

"I would imagine that saving your friend's life is priceless. But this is a fair exchange, and one cancels the other. Now pay." Smoke swirled around him, lashing out in wisps.

Marcus opened his mouth to speak, but shut it again.

Fairday's thoughts were racing. "What do you want from us?"

"I require payment from the girl. A token." He extended a dark hand toward Lizzy.

"I don't have anything!" Lizzy's voice quivered.

Laughing low, the Shadow Rook answered, "Everyone has something."

Lizzy looked over at Marcus and Fairday.

Marcus spoke up. "Hey, look, mister. We have some stuff in our backpacks. Not money or anything, but maybe there's something you'll like. Take what you want and leave her alone."

"A token from the girl is required to cover the debt," the cold voice said.

Fairday's mind skipped to Ruby Begonia. She'd been tricked by Eldrich into trading her beauty and song for magical sneakers that didn't fit. Remembering the outcome of that story gave her the courage to speak up. "What kind of token?"

"Whatever she has to give," the Shadow Rook said, and even without a face, Fairday could feel his evil grin.

"I told you, I don't have anything!" Lizzy said. Her voice rose and her face flushed deep pink.

"Be careful, Lizzy. This is like Ruby's deal with Eldrich," Fairday said.

"What happens if I don't pay?"

"You will grow dimmer until all that remains is shadows."

"How can you do that?" Marcus asked.

"It is the law of the library. Thieves pay the Rook or pay the price. I do not make the rules. Now, what will you give me?"

Lizzy was silent for a moment, then asked, "Can I talk with my friends?"

"I see no reason why not. Time means nothing to me." He slunk back and turned away.

Fairday and Marcus huddled around Lizzy, bending in to whisper.

"What're we gonna do? I don't want to give up anything about myself—look what happened to Ruby!"

"I know," Fairday whispered. "We've been misled, for sure. This whole thing feels like a trap."

"But how are we going to get past this guy? Lizzy has to give him something or she'll turn into a shadow," Marcus said.

"Lizzy, do you have anything on you?" Fairday asked.

"Just my bobby pin." Pulling it out of her front pocket and holding it up, she said, "But I don't think he'll want this."

Fairday thought for a minute. "He didn't say what he wanted, only that it had to be from you. Your hair is something that's unique."

"I don't want to lose my hair!" Lizzy grasped her head.

"I don't think you'll lose your hair. But you use that; I'm sure he'll take it."

"How can you know?" Marcus asked.

"In stories, spells and magic always require something personal from the victim in order to work," Fairday said. In an even quieter voice, she said, "Listen, I think we've been set up, and someone is trying to stop us from helping Fas capture the bookworm. We have to get out of here and back to the Begonia House, or we'll wind up in even deeper trouble!"

"Yeah, where is Fas anyway? Isn't this *his* library?" Marcus asked.

"Maybe something's happened to him, and he's in trouble too," Lizzy said.

"Right, we have no idea what's going on. We should give the Rook what he wants, then get back to finding our way home," Fairday said.

Marcus nodded.

"Okay, I'll give him my bobby pin, but I'm really nervous," Lizzy said.

They stood up and Marcus called out, "Hey, Shadow Rook. Time to get paid."

The darkness shifted and he appeared. "A well-thought-out choice, I presume." The Shadow Rook extended his arm.

"Here you go." Lizzy dropped the bobby pin onto his hand.

"Very good," the Shadow Rook cooed as the pin sunk into the darkness of his palm. A spark shot out, lighting up his form for an instant. Suddenly, Lizzy's hair fell flat.

Fairday could hear her friend stifle a sob and felt anger rising again. "We've paid you, now leave," she said.

"Ah yes. The price has been met. I thank you kindly."
The Shadow Rook turned and headed toward the other side
of the hearth.

"I wonder what that means," Lizzy replied, blowing
the limp strands away from her eyes.

"It's like your bobby pin turned into smoke or something,"
Marcus said. "You do look pretty weird with straight hair."

"Thanks, Marcus. Way to kick me when I'm down."

"I didn't say it was bad, it's different, but still cool."

"So we're back to square one," Fairday said.

"**HARMFUL** was right. The riddle was a trick,"
Marcus said.

"I don't think it was *all* a trick," Lizzy said.

"What do you mean?" Marcus asked.

"Well, I think Fas meant for us to find USEFUL. That
would make sense. The information we were looking for
was in that book. I think Alice was purposely misleading
us with her clue about the fireplace."

"I agree," Fairday said. "But that's how we found out
about the mirror."

"True," Marcus said.

"Yeah, but maybe touching that side activated an
alarm, alerting the Shadow Rook, or maybe that part of
the riddle was a warning. What did it say?"

Marcus piped up. "'What you see isn't here.'"

"Exactly! I'm pretty sure Alice set us up to get caught," Lizzy said.

"But why?" Fairday asked.

"That's the question," Lizzy answered. "All the circumstances are suspicious. The smudged writing. The book falling from out of nowhere. Alice acting crazy. I mean, it all fits."

"You don't think the riddle was a trick?" Marcus asked.

"Nope." Lizzy shook her head. "The house's magic seems to work in riddles. I think we should start from there."

"That brings us back to needing the ruby. It's too dangerous to poke around the tower, so how are we gonna get it out?" Marcus asked.

Fairday's brain was whirring. There must be something that could point them in the right direction. Out of the corner of her eye, she noticed *Interesting* perched on top of the castle tower. The book's catlike eyes were slowly following the question mark dragonfly along its edge. In a flash, the book pounced, crunching wings between toothy pages. A light bulb went off in Fairday's head. She looked at her partners, and said, "I have an idea."

~ Fifteen ~
WHICH PART WORKS?

"We have to get the punctuation to work for us," Fairday said.

"What?" Marcus asked.

"Look around this place, it's everywhere." Fairday gestured to a set of commas spinning a thread up the queen's nose. One dangled off the tip, while the other struggled to climb higher.

"We can't risk getting poisoned. Plus we don't want to meet up with the Rook again." Marcus shot a glance at Lizzy.

"We don't have to touch the punctuation bugs, just get them to help us."

"Eh?" Marcus said.

"Oh! I get it!" Lizzy said. "So *they* get the ruby."

"That's what I'm thinking. The Shadow Rook said, 'All parts of a story work for their master, if the master knows the parts of a story,'" Fairday said.

"Let me try," Lizzy said. She stood up, held her hands out like a band conductor, and announced, "Quotes gather together and form a circle." Nothing happened. She shrugged.

Fairday twisted her hands. "I'm sure this is the answer, but maybe it's more complicated. Each punctuation mark has a purpose, which must tie into it somehow."

"What about: punctuation, obey our every command, period!" Marcus blurted out.

Lizzy threw him a look.

"I mean, if we say the right words to the right punctuation marks, I think they'd listen, because it'd serve their purpose," Fairday said.

"Huh? You lost me." Marcus scratched his head.

"Hang on, let me write it down." Fairday walked over to her pack and pulled out the notebook. Picking up the pen from the floor, she sat cross-legged, flipped to a blank page, then began to write: Commas pause. Periods stop. Quotes speak. *What else?* Her thoughts quickened as she wrote, question marks ask. As she reread her words, they sparked an idea.

"Well?" Marcus and Lizzy said, looking at Fairday.

Fairday grinned back at them. "I know what to do." She jumped up and turned to face the hallways of books. Speaking to the room, she asked, "Why did the question mark get the ruby?"

From out of nowhere, a flurry of wings descended upon them. Lizzy crouched and grabbed Marcus's sleeve. Fairday held her breath. She could feel buzzing all around her and knew her plan was working. *She had their attention!*

"What's happening, Fairday?" Lizzy whispered.

"A question mark would want to know, that's their part in a story," Fairday said, then spoke out again. "Bring me the ruby, and I'll tell you the answer."

The cloud hovered for a moment, then some scattered. Fairday felt her stomach clench. Could she be wrong? *This had to be it!* A few remained, circling. Suddenly, they darted into the castle tower and, moments later, emerged carrying the jewel. The ruby zipped through the air on vibrating wings, then stopped in front of Fairday. She held out her hand. "The answer is because I asked you to." The question marks dropped the stone, then flew off.

"This must be your Wordcaster abilities coming through," Marcus said.

"That was brilliant," Lizzy said, smiling.

Fairday beamed at her friends. "Now let's get out of here." They whipped on their backpacks, then turned their attention to the stone court. Feeling ready for anything, Fairday held up the ruby, then set it in the queen's scepter.

The jewel began to glow and the stones shook. A crack split down the fireplace. The statues parted and a dark passage was revealed.

"Are we really going in there?" Fairday's voice quivered.

"Let's link arms, so we stick together," Lizzy suggested.

Marcus nodded, and they grasped onto each other before walking in. Fairday looked at the queen's face as she passed by. Her blank eyes gave away no secrets. Without warning, the stones shifted behind them, sealing the hearth.

"Oh no!" Fairday stepped back.

"Wait." Lizzy squeezed her arm. "Let's see what happens."

On her right, Marcus tightened his grip. Fairday held her breath as the path began to glow pale green. Soft light flooded the area and she could see sparks flickering ahead. The air felt warmer and smelled like the woods; birds chirped above a low-buzzing hum. *Where were they?*

"Shall we?" Marcus extended an arm into the unknown.

"Should we click our heels first?" Fairday asked, reminded of her favorite book.

"You betcha," Lizzy said. "And repeat, 'There's no place like home.'"

The DMS took a united step forward, deeper into the mystery.

~ Sixteen ~

THE COMMON DOOR

A breeze touched Fairday's cheeks as leafy plants sprang up around them and sunlight filtered through a canopy of trees, speckling the forest underbrush.

"This doesn't seem too scary," Lizzy said.

"Yet," Marcus muttered and peered through the trees.

As their journey began, Fairday felt like she was on familiar ground, but couldn't figure out why. The path went on, twisting through woods. Off in the distance, she saw something that made her jump for joy. "Look! It's the willow tree. I can see the third-floor balcony too."

"You betcha! That's the willow." Lizzy's voice fell. "Only it's in bloom. Everything is. That can't be, it's October."

"This must be outside the *other* side of the Begonia House," Marcus said.

"We found the common door USEFUL told us about! It's the one in the mirror on the third floor. Which means we'll get back home. You were right, Lizzy." Fairday beamed at her friend.

"That must be it! And now we know what's outside. We definitely need to make a map of this place at some point," Lizzy said.

"I think I'm getting the hang of it," Marcus said. "But a map would be nice to add to the blueprints. Your house is pretty intense, Fairday."

"I know, right?" Fairday grinned.

"Hey! Maybe we'll see the ghosts at Ruby's wedding again," Marcus said as he turned and jogged ahead.

"That'll be interesting." Lizzy ran to catch up.

The path led to Fairday's backyard and ended at the edge of the woods. The willow tree swayed peacefully, and its leaves twinkled in the sun.

"You'd never suspect that tree's so sinister," Lizzy said.

Fairday remembered how it had come to life and tried to grab them. She shuddered. Thank goodness *that* problem had been solved.

"I think we should check it out."

"You always want to go to the tree, Marcus," Lizzy teased.

"Hey! That's where the blueprints were hidden. I know where to find the clues."

The three detectives crept up to the willow. As they drew near, Fairday thought it looked like a mysterious lady dressed in a gown of green. Lizzy pulled aside the curtain-like branches, and they ducked underneath. The gnarled trunk rose high, leaves dangling around them.

The DMS spread out around the base, looking for anything odd. Feeling the bark with her fingertips, Fairday's eyes scanned the tree.

"I don't see anything," Marcus said. "There's nothing sticking out of the trunk."

"Good we checked," Lizzy said, patting his back.

They peered out into the yard. The ghost people were there, chatting among themselves, forever frolicking. Out of the corner of her eye, Fairday noticed something that didn't quite fit. A bird was perched on the balcony railing, watching over the scene. It looked like a crow, except it had black-and-white feathers.

"Look up there," Fairday whispered.

"The bird?" Lizzy asked.

"Something's weird about it."

Marcus flung off his pack and yanked out the infrared goggles. Aiming them, he said, "It glows, so it's giving off heat. Must be alive."

Lizzy tugged on Fairday's sleeve. "Let's get out of here. I don't think the bird or the ghost people are going to bother us."

"Okay," Fairday said, and they made their way up to the house. The guests at the party carried on. No one took any notice as they passed by, except two beady eyes spying from above.

⌇ Seventeen ⌇
THE MIRROR REMEMBERS

The three sleuths creaked open the double doors of the Begonia House. Everything looked as it had the last time they'd been on this side. The black-and-white checkered floor gleamed under the chandelier, and the smell of roses filled the air.

On her way down the second-floor hallway, Fairday stopped at the portrait of Cora Lynn Begonia and looked into her eyes.

"Can you still see the hallway on your side of the house?" Lizzy asked.

"Yes, which is awesome. No one's there right now." It did make Fairday feel slightly better knowing there were a few places on this side of the house where she could check in on what was happening in real time on her side. Her family was never too far away!

Opening the door to the third floor, they walked up the spiral staircase. Rounding the top, they faced the mirror. Luckily, the reflection showed Fairday's side, with the broken wall sconce and dangling bulb. *They were almost home!*

"In our last case we needed the brass key to open the door in the mirror," Fairday said. "But it's locked in the wardrobe with the blueprints."

A door appeared behind the glass.

"Whoa! I love when it's easy." Marcus grinned.

"You don't think this is *too* easy?" Lizzy sounded skeptical. "We know the key unlocked the mirror's magic and opened the portal."

"We've earned it! Maybe we've proven ourselves to the house." Marcus clapped his hands together.

"But we know the wardrobe works, and all we have to do is knock the right sequence. We could—" Fairday's words were cut short as Marcus let out a whooping yell and leaped into the mirror.

Lizzy shrugged. "I guess that's the plan," she said, and jumped in after him.

Fairday was about to follow when she heard someone whispering her name. Walking over, she looked down the spiral staircase. No one was there. Shaking it off, she turned and approached the mirror, but the door inside it closed.

Shadows crept over the reflection in the mirror, extending from the twisted vines around the edge. Fairday's body tensed as she watched. The door opened, but her friends weren't there. Instead she saw Fas, unconscious and tied up, being shoved by a large man wearing a cap and grimy clothes. Fairday couldn't see the man's face, but noticed dark hair and a tattoo on the back of his neck. The stranger pushed hard, and Fas tumbled down the spiral staircase. Her heart dropped as she leaped forward, yelling, "No!"

The door shut and the shadows retreated. When it opened again, Lizzy and Marcus were on the other side. Feeling shaken, Fairday stepped through the glass. *It was all true. The Librarian had been double-crossed, and all the stories would be lost. Life without books?* Fairday didn't want to think about it.

"Fas is in trouble," Fairday said after she came out of the mirror, relieved to finally be on her side of the house. "The door shut and the reflection changed before I could come through. It showed him knocked out and tied up, then a strange man pushed him."

"Oh no! That's terrible!" Lizzy covered her mouth with her hand. "I wonder what's happened to Sanir?"

"This is really serious," Fairday said. "If we don't solve this case, stories will be forever changed. We have to set it right!"

"So what's the next step?" Marcus asked.

"I want to check the blueprints. They're in here." Fairday went into DMS headquarters.

Lizzy and Marcus followed. The rose pattern on the stained glass window gave the space a pink glow. Fairday had dusted and gotten rid of some of the junk left behind by the Begonias, but there were still boxes and newspapers in the corners. Her dad had brought up an old desk, and she'd set it up with their folders and notes.

"Headquarters looks nice!" Marcus said and stretched out on the striped chair.

Fairday walked over to the wardrobe. Before unlocking it, she unwrapped her hand and checked the cut. It had stopped bleeding. "I'll have my mom wash this for you. Thanks for lending it to me," she said and set Lizzy's headband on the desk.

"No problem, glad I could help." Lizzy smiled.

Fairday turned her attention on the wardrobe. She used the secret code and knocked three times, then three more. The iron claws unclasped, and she pulled out the silver canister.

Fairday uncorked the top and rolled the blueprints out on the floor.

"What're you looking for?" Lizzy asked.

"Information about the mirror." Fairday flipped through the pages. "I want to know why it showed me Fas being captured." She scanned the words written around the sketch of the mirror.

"Here's the answer!" Fairday poked the bottom of the page and read aloud, *"Between the glass is the common door, where two worlds meet forevermore. Once the mirror sees what's known, it remembers all it's shown. To recollect times gone by, call upon the smart magpie. Should you need a tell-on-you, the reflection will provide the clue."*

"What's a magpie?" Lizzy asked.

"No idea," Fairday said.

Marcus shrugged.

"Fas was worried that something sinister was going on. I bet he fixed it ahead of time so the mirror would show us what happened." Fairday rolled up the blueprints, then corked the canister. Placing them back in the wardrobe, she shut the door, knocked three times, plus four, and the sequence caused the claws to clasp.

"Yeah, that makes sense. Looks like we're on our own," Marcus said.

"Well, we know we need to talk to Ruby to find out—" Lizzy stopped and tilted her head. "Is that your mom, Fairday?"

"Kids! Are you up there?"

Fairday ran to the door and flung it open. "We're in here, Mom."

Auntie Em was with her, barking like mad. "Thank goodness you're okay!" Mrs. Morrow was out of breath. "When I couldn't find you, I thought something terrible must've happened." She put her hand to her chest.

"What's wrong?" Fairday asked, eyebrows furrowed.

"You didn't feel the earthquake a few minutes ago?" Her mom's voice rose. Auntie Em circled her feet, whimpering and sniffing.

Earthquake? Could that've been what they'd felt when the Talking Library had shaken and *Alice in Wonderland* fell at their feet? Marcus had thought so, but that had happened ages ago. Did time slow down in the library? Or did it speed up? All she knew was it was different!

"Marcus and Lizzy, you should call your parents, they're probably worried. You can use the phone in the foyer."

"Thanks," they said and headed downstairs.

"Dad and Margo are okay, right?" Fairday asked, the pit in her stomach growing.

"They're fine. Dad's a bit worked up. He's on his cell with Grandma." She took a deep breath and refastened her curly brown hair into her clip. "Always an adventure around this place." Frowning, she added, "Odd that you didn't feel the house shake up here. I wonder how that's possible?"

"No clue," Fairday said. "This whole place is one big mystery."

"You should see the plans to fix the plumbing." Her mom pulled her in for a hug. "Come on. Your dad's been cooking. Let's get something to eat, and you can give me the latest scoop."

"I don't think you can handle it, Mom." Fairday grinned. She couldn't imagine what her parents would think if they knew about all the secrets the Begonia House was keeping.

"You'd be surprised at the things I can handle, honey," Mrs. Morrow said. She patted Fairday's shoulder as they climbed down the spiral stairs. Auntie Em led the way, stubby tail wagging. Fairday hadn't realized how hungry she was. Any snack prepared by her dad would hit the spot! After all, he was a wizard in the kitchen and had the power to charm her taste buds!

∾ Eighteen ∾
FEELING UP TO PAR?

Mrs. Morrow pushed through the swinging kitchen doors and Fairday followed the scent of rosemary. Margo was in her high chair and her dad was standing at the stove, talking on his cell. He smiled at Fairday and squeezed Mrs. Morrow's shoulder as she walked by. He ended his call, then bent down to pull a pan out of the oven.

Fairday's stomach growled as she sat down at the table. Everything seemed normal here. She took a breath and relaxed.

"Farfey! Shaky, shaky!" Margo said, squeezing her stuffed pony, Mr. Fazzy.

"I know! Mom said you were very brave," Fairday said.

"That's right, poopsykins." Mrs. Morrow kissed the end of Margo's nose and sat down next to her.

Margo shoved a handful of cereal in her mouth, dropping half on the floor. Auntie Em was on top of it, and they were gone in an instant.

Lizzy came in and pulled out the chair next to Fairday. "Everything's all set with my parents." She scrunched up her face, pretending to pinch Margo. "You betcha, I'll getcha!"

Margo squealed and threw cornflakes in the air. Auntie Em was having a *very* good day.

Marcus appeared next through the swinging doors. "My dad said they didn't feel much, only a slight tremor."

"They barely felt anything? That's weird." Mrs. Morrow's brow furrowed.

Marcus nodded. "Of course, an earthquake doesn't stop me from having to rake the yard before dinner. So I've gotta run."

"Raking—that stinks," Lizzy said. "Have fun."

"Thanks for your support." Marcus winked at her.

"Anytime." Lizzy smirked. Sniffing the air, she asked, "Fairday, are those your dad's famous fries I smell?"

"Made in your honor, *mademoiselle!*" Mr. Morrow said and placed a plate in front of Lizzy. Looking her over, he stepped back and tapped his chin. "Hmm, I've never seen your hair quite so straight. If I didn't know better, I'd say the earthquake shook the curls right out."

Lizzy muffled a cough. "No, ha ha. *That'd* be wild. I'm just trying a new hairstyle." Snatching a fry, she gestured to Marcus. "Have one of these before you go. Mr.

Morrow is a celebrity for this recipe with our friends in New York. It's a real treat!"

Marcus grabbed a fry, then dipped it in the sauce. He closed his eyes, chewing. "Whoa! These are amazing!"

"They're parsnips," Lizzy said.

"Par—what?"

"Par-snips. You know, the vegetable. It looks like a carrot, but whitish. French fry flavor, only way healthier." She smacked her lips. "I *love* them!"

Marcus took another. "These are awesome, but I have to go." Turning to Fairday and Lizzy, he said, "You have my number. Keep me posted."

"We will! Bye!"

Mr. Morrow saluted him. "So long, brave sir. May the handle of your rake remain true on your mission to organize nature."

"Thanks. I hope it goes fast," Marcus said and left the kitchen. A moment later, the front door banged shut.

The girls finished up the last of the fries and Lizzy filled Fairday in on what was happening at her old school. The phone rang and Mr. Morrow left the kitchen to answer it. Lizzy continued, "— which means now we may not get to go on the field trip. Everyone's upset."

"I can imagine." Fairday remembered how much she'd been looking forward to the annual fifth-grade class trip before she'd moved.

Mr. Morrow strode in and ran a hand through his hair. "That was Mr. Lovell on the phone. He asked us to brunch at his house tomorrow."

Fairday and Lizzy exchanged glances. Larry Lovell had helped them solve their last case, and Fairday hoped they could count on him now. Plus it was the perfect chance to talk to Ruby.

"An interesting turn of events!" Mr. Morrow announced. "Well, gang, whadda ya say?"

Margo grinned, banging her bowl in approval.

"Excellent!" Fairday said. "Sunday will be full of surprises."

"You can say that again." Lizzy nodded.

"I had a delightful time talking with him last week, and I'd love to pick his brain about what this place was like back in its heyday." Mrs. Morrow gestured to the kitchen with its worn appliances and cracked floor.

Mr. Morrow clapped his hands. "Wonderful. It's a date. Now, girls, I have some work to do, and Mom's going to be busy on the phone with the contractors. With all the excitement, we'd prefer it if you two stick around where I can see you."

"Sure, Dad," Fairday said. *She needed a break!* "We'll play Harry Potter Trivia in here until dinner. I'll go get it."

"That's a brilliant idea!" Lizzy said.

Fairday walked to the front closet to get the Harry Potter Prefect edition, one of their favorite ways to pass time. After having such a crazy day, a game would calm things down a bit. They were going to need their brains sharp in order to piece together this puzzle!

Reaching up to grab it off the shelf, she thought about retired journalist Larry Lovell. Interviewing him for school, she'd found out about his connection to the Begonia family, which had helped the DMS solve the last case. He'd come to their aid once they'd found Ruby and was there when the enchantment broke. It hadn't been easy explaining who Ruby was to her parents during Sunday dinner. They'd managed a convincing story on the fly, and Ruby went to stay at Larry's house. Fairday wondered how she was doing now. Larry seemed like a nice older gentleman, but would he be able to take care of her? Fairday hoped so. That poor lady deserved to be happy after being locked up for so long.

Heading back to the kitchen, Fairday sidestepped a paint can. Brunch tomorrow had possibilities, and she hoped Ruby and Larry had some answers up their sleeves.

~ Nineteen ~
ADDING UP THE CLUES

The electric lantern cast a glow in the makeshift tent the girls had made in DMS headquarters. With Fairday's bedroom off limits, it was the perfect place to set up camp.

Sitting cross-legged and bundled in blankets, they finally had a moment to sort everything out.

Fairday's notebook was flipped open and the girls jotted down what they knew so far. They racked their brains to make connections, but nothing clicked.

MYSTERY: A bookworm is loose and eating words in stories
MISSION: Find Eldrich and bring her to the Talking Library (TL)
LEAD: Ruby Begonia-Larry Lovell's house Sunday

Interviewing Ruby was the next step. Would she help them find Eldrich? Fairday hoped Ruby could give them some answers. How long did it take the bookworm to devour words? She had no idea. One thing was for sure, time *didn't* feel like it was on their side, and so far there wasn't any evidence that came even close to solving the case. Fairday wasn't sure if they'd be able to figure it out before more important words were eaten. Mind buzzing, her eyes reread their notes:

Spider/Sanir led us to hatch under grand staircase

    —Lizzy can understand it w/ the sneakers

Fell down hatch/saw 3 windows:

    —1st: roses/silver spoon

    —2nd: closed blinds/ticking clock

    (blinds open- giant eye/shadow figures)

    —3rd: broken glass/colored jars

Riddle for TL - purple potion w/ jars and spoon

    —sang Purple People Eater/door on dock vanished

Storykeepers like Anansi / spirit of stories/trickster

    —Fas, Librarian of TL

    —Sanir, his son

TL - books can talk to you/smell and go in story

    (first editions kept there)

Ruby was a "Housekeeper" - link to human mind, kept portal safe

    —she doesn't know about TL

    —books showed a riddle clue /smudged note to ask Alice

Alice came during earthquake / happened here too, but later

    —how does time work in TL?

Fire was a reflection - was Alice's clue a trick?

Statues behind hearth - pieces switched/gem locked up

Lizzy bit by poisonous punctuation - a setup?

Shadow Rook saved Lizzy, gave him her bobby pin

—hair flat - WHY?

Fireplace leads outside other side of the Begonia House

Mirror is the door between the two worlds

—it remembers what it reflects - see blueprints

WHO KIDNAPPED FAS???

—man: dirty clothes, cap, dark hair, tattoo on neck

What's a magpie?

Make a map!

Fairday closed the notebook, setting it aside. Turning to Lizzy, she said, "Well, we've got plenty to go on, but nothing makes sense."

"You betcha." Lizzy yawned and snuggled into the blankets.

"I guess we'd better get some sleep. Tomorrow's going to be busy," Fairday said. But Lizzy was already snoring.

Switching off the light, she got comfortable and stared at the darkness for a while, her mind spinning like a carousel. Lizzy never had trouble drifting off into dreamland, and Fairday envied her. Sleep eventually came, but instead of peace, it brought strange and turbulent dreams, which seemed all too real.

❧ Twenty ❧
BRUNCH AND A HUNCH

The Morrow family cruiser rumbled down the long driveway to Larry Lovell's. Fairday peered out the window at passing fields and grazing cows. As the car rounded a corner, an old farmhouse appeared.

Mr. Morrow parked the car and everyone piled out; Margo squirmed in her seat.

"Alright, snookykins. Upsidaisy," Mrs. Morrow cooed and unbuckled the straps.

Mr. Morrow led the way, carrying a quiche and a basket of blueberry muffins. He rang the bell, and they waited. After a few minutes he shrugged, then knocked.

"H'llo? Who's there?" came a gruff voice from the other side.

"The Morrow family plus one, sir!"

Larry Lovell opened the door. Fairday hid a smile. *He always looked so grumpy.*

"Come, come." He waved them in with his cane.

The smell of coffee was inviting as they followed Larry's clicking steps down a hall. Fairday tried to get the scope of the place and noticed newspaper clippings hung on the walls, but before she could catch a headline, they'd reached the dining room.

Steaming dishes stretched out on a table with a bench lining one side and chairs on the other. Larry took his seat, then said, "Please, sit. Find a spot that looks good to you."

As Fairday slid onto the bench, she noticed Ruby wasn't there. Lizzy squeezed in next to Fairday, and the look on her face said she was thinking the same thing.

Larry hooked his cane on the back of his chair. "Hm, mm." He cleared his throat. "I don't entertain often, so thank you for coming." He looked down the table at them.

"We appreciate the invitation," Mrs. Morrow said, settling Margo in her booster seat.

"It's great to see you again, Mr. Lovell," Fairday spoke up.

"You as well, and your friend too, Lizzy, if I'm correct?"

"That's me." Lizzy beamed at him.

"I had a hunch I'd catch you two together again. In this case, better sooner than later."

Fairday felt Lizzy pinch her under the table. *Did Larry know something?*

"If you're up to spinning a yarn, we'd love to listen," Mr. Morrow said.

"Hm, mm. I've plenty to tell. But first, regarding my house guest, she apologizes for her absence. She enjoyed meeting the girls last week at dinner and would like them to stop by her room for a visit after they've eaten. If it's okay with you folks, that is."

Fairday's heart skipped a beat and she crossed her fingers.

Mr. and Mrs. Morrow exchanged glances.

"I think that's a fine idea," Mr. Morrow concluded with a nod.

"Very well then, let's dig in," Larry said and passed the rolls to Lizzy.

Fairday filled her plate as the food traveled around. Her brain spun with questions. Would Ruby be happy to see them after everything that had happened? Being trapped alone on the other side of the Begonia House for so long had made her behavior a bit loopy. Fairday remembered her wild red hair and flashing green eyes when she and Lizzy had first seen her in the mirror. Ruby had been watching them from the other side of the house. After they'd captured her, she'd been raging like a caged animal. Fairday noticed she'd stuffed her feet into the high-heeled sneakers, even though they didn't fit. It was like she'd been torturing herself. Hopefully, Ruby felt cheerier now that her wish to leave the Begonia House had been granted.

After brunch, Larry excused the girls and sent them to Ruby's room. On their way, an article caught Fairday's eye and she tugged Lizzy's sleeve.

"Look at this," she said, pointing to the wall.

Lizzy read the headline. "'Begonia Estate Donates Rare Private Collection.' Interesting. Wonder what it was?"

"No clue, but it seems important." Fairday scanned the small print. Nothing popped out at her, but there was no time to read. Ruby was expecting them.

"You're gonna be *so* proud of me." Lizzy took the camera out of her front pocket, then snapped a picture. "Got it!"

"Nice work." Fairday patted her partner on the back.

Following Larry's directions, they walked up the stairs and stopped at the third door.

Fairday whispered, "Remember, she's probably still shaken up."

"We should try not to upset her, which might not be easy." Lizzy pushed her hair back. "Okay, let's do it."

Fairday took a breath, then knocked on Ruby's door.

Twenty One
MIXED MEANINGS

"I'm here," a muffled voice spoke from inside.

Fairday opened the door to find Ruby wearing a pink nightgown. She was staring out the window in a rocking chair, twisting a lace curtain in her lap.

"Hi, Ruby," Lizzy said.

The girls walked over. Ruby wasn't scary anymore; her red hair was mostly gray now, and she seemed withdrawn. She tilted her head and said, "Oh, hello. Can I help you?"

"Mr. Lovell said you wanted to see us," Fairday said.

"He did. Did he?" She began to rock harder.

"Yeah. Is that alright?"

The chair stopped short and Ruby glared at them. "Nothing to do about it now. Unless you choose to leave, that is. A much more powerful choice than most realize. *I* should know."

"Do you want us to go?" Fairday asked. She could understand if Ruby wasn't up to visitors yet. It had only been a week since her sudden freedom, and the world had changed over the last fifty years.

Ruby's silence was awkward until she dropped the lace and said, "No. Larry wants me to talk to you. At the very least, I owe him that. He's been so nice." She sighed, hanging her head.

Fairday and Lizzy sat on the edge of the bed, eager to hear her story.

"I kept a secret from you the last time we met." Ruby's green eyes shifted as she spoke. "I didn't tell you about the magpie—my bird, that is."

The girls glanced at each other. *A magpie was a bird!*

"I told you I was alone on the other side of the house, but that wasn't entirely true. I had a pet of sorts, a magpie who called himself Edgar."

"The bird called itself a name?" Lizzy asked.

"He wasn't an ordinary bird." Ruby's fingers started to fidget. "He could talk."

"Lots of birds talk. My friend has a parrot that can say over a hundred words," Lizzy said.

"Not like this one. Edgar was very clever, and"—she paused—"he'd bring me things."

"Where'd you find him?"

"After I became a prisoner of the house, I spent hours on the balcony, watching the ghosts at my wedding. One day a black-and-white bird perched next to me. I shooed it away, but it came back." Ruby paused, her reflection staring in the glass. "I rushed inside, but the bird pecked at the window. So I threw it open and screamed, hoping to scare it off. Instead, it flew in and landed on the mirror."

"What'd you do?"

Ruby eyed Lizzy. "I closed the door to my room and waited. Of course, it wasn't long before curiosity won over fear, and I looked out. The bird hadn't moved, so I left the door open and sat on my bed. Then, it told me its name was Edgar."

Fairday felt a chill as she imagined the scene. *How creepy!*

"I was terrified and slammed the door. But what could I do? Hiding was only delaying the inevitable. So I faced the bird and told him my name."

"Then he became your pet?" Lizzy scrunched up her nose.

"No. He flew away. But a week later, he returned to tell me a riddle." Ruby closed her eyes, then recited, "A thing in mind can't be found, but may still come around. Speak it out and you shall see this or that brought to thee."

"What's it mean?"

"What do *you* think it means?" Ruby's eyes focused on Fairday.

The words rolled around her brain like marbles. *That's an analogy, Fairday,* her dad's voice piped in. There were no marbles in her head, but the thought of them *was* a thing in her mind. The idea inspired her answer. "Did Edgar want you to ask for something?"

"Clever girl, that's correct." Ruby nodded.

"What'd you choose?"

"I thought Eldrich desired *more* from me than she'd already stolen; her magic worked by mixed meanings. But what else could she take? The only thing I wanted was freedom, and no bird could give me that, so I chose my father's writing pen. He used to say ink was the blood of wild thought."

"And the bird brought it to you?"

"Yes," Ruby answered. "Every now and then Edgar returned to tell a riddle and bring me gifts. I never found out how he got them, but I was so grateful for the company." A tear slid down her cheek. "Until now, that is."

"Why? What happened?"

Ruby's gaze shifted. "Just before your family moved into the house, Edgar brought me a manifest of my father's private book collection. His estate had donated it to the Ashpot Library months before, and it was open for public viewing."

The girls shot each other a look. *Could that be what the article was about?*

"Is that what Mr. Lovell wanted you to tell us?" Fairday asked.

"Not exactly. You see, Edgar recently came *here*. I was delighted—until he spoke."

"What'd he say?"

"He said, 'Odds are neither here nor there. If they come, tell them where.'"

"What are Odds?"

"They're what my father called his hidden treasures."

"Do you know where they are?" *The blue glass ball—it must be one of Thurston's Odds!* He had used it to contact Eldrich, and now it could be the key to helping Fas stop the bookworm.

"I won't tell you." Ruby scowled. "Edgar *is* working for that evil hag, and now she's using you to get what she wants."

Fairday understood her anger. Fas must have sent the bird to help them, but Ruby thought Eldrich was playing tricks again. Would they be able to gain her trust?

"If you tell us where the Odds are, we'll bring them to you," Lizzy said.

"No, I don't want them. I wish to be alone." Ruby dismissed them with a wave.

As they turned to leave, she spoke again. "But since you helped me, I will tell you this: their whereabouts are written in a book."

"Will you give us the title?" Fairday asked.

"No," Ruby said. "*That* secret's safe in my old room."

Fairday glanced at Lizzy. *Ruby just told them where to look!*

"Thanks, Ruby. Bye," Lizzy said and walked out.

Silence followed, but as Fairday shut the door, Ruby said, "Larry *can't* be right."

∿ Twenty Two ∾
PLOTTING PLANS

On the car ride home, Mr. and Mrs. Morrow chatted while Margo bounced in her seat. The girls couldn't talk about the case, so Fairday listened, watching out the window. The orange, red, and yellow foliage blurred by like her racing thoughts; Ruby's words circled in her mind. *What wasn't Larry right about? Clueing them in on Edgar? Or did he know something else?*

"Well, Fairday?"

"Sorry, Dad, didn't catch that."

"I was saying that Mr. Lovell wanted me to remind you to bring along the books when you meet him at the Ashpot Library this Tuesday. He seemed to think I'd be dropping you off there after school." Mr. Morrow raised an eyebrow in the rearview mirror. "Is this for a project you're working on?"

Fairday hid her surprise. "Yeah. Sorry, I forgot to ask. Mr. Lovell said he'd help me with research for class." *That sounded logical!*

"Well, I'm happy to play a part in your quest for knowledge."

"Thanks, Dad," Fairday said, not sure what was happening at the library. Larry must've set things up for a reason. She hoped he'd have information about the case, but Fas said Ruby didn't even know about the Talking Library, so how likely was it that Larry did? He had written more than one article about the Begonia House and its occupants, but he'd had no clue about the parallel world until he saw Ruby. No, he couldn't know anything about it. It had to be something else. The suspense was driving her crazy.

As the cruiser pulled up to the Begonia House, Fairday saw a blue sports car parked in the circular drive; Mr. Mackerville leaned against it, talking on his cell.

"Lizzy, I didn't know your father would be here," Mrs. Morrow said.

"That's weird. I thought my brother was coming," Lizzy said, shooting Fairday a nervous glance across the backseat.

Mr. Morrow cut the engine and stepped out of the car. Extending his hand, he said, "Good to see you, Garth. Hope we haven't kept you waiting." Both men were tall, but otherwise very different. Garth Mackerville practically lived in suits, and her dad, well, sometimes he wore his "Got Food" apron to the store.

"Not at all," Mr. Mackerville said. He nodded at Mrs. Morrow. "Pru."

"Garth," Mrs. Morrow said, scooching Margo up on her hip. "Excuse me, I've got to get this one down for her nap. Right, poopsykins?" She hurried up the steps, into the house.

"Hello, Lizzy." Mr. Mackerville hugged her. "I like what you've done with your hair."

"Thanks." Lizzy smoothed it down. "I'm still getting used to my new do."

"Mark asked me to pick you up. If we leave now we'll beat traffic. Your mom's expecting us by five. Your Aunt Forsey's in town from Minnesota." He checked his watch.

"OMG! That's so exciting!" Lizzy beamed.

Lizzy absolutely loved her aunt. Whenever she and Lizzy drank pink lemonade, they'd make a toast to fun Aunt Forsey.

"Are you packed?" Mr. Mackerville asked.

"Yep, I'll go grab my stuff. Come on!" Lizzy pulled on Fairday's sleeve, and they raced into the house. Auntie Em barked as the girls rushed through the front door.

Upstairs, Lizzy gathered her things. "Well, it's going to be a busy week. There's a ton to figure out, so I'll check my email for updates."

"I'll keep you posted. I'm searching Ruby's room later."

"Be careful, Fairday. Things *are not* what they seem in this house."

Fairday nodded, and the girls skipped downstairs. Auntie Em was by the front door.

"Later, sausage!" Lizzy patted the pug's head. Turning to Fairday, she added, "I'm *so* excited for the boo—k party on Saturday! After today's adventures my character costume will be even more fitting."

"My dad's going all out with the scary decor this year, so it's sure to be one for the record books. The Begonia House is the perfect place to have it."

"You betcha."

They walked up to their dads, who were still talking by the car.

"Interesting place, Patrick. Could be a wise investment," Mr. Mackerville said.

"Garth, let me tell you." Mr. Morrow ran a hand through his hair. "We followed our hearts and *voila*! A dream made tangible."

"But the money will make it all worthwhile."

"If more than bread dough is baking, then bonus points."

"Thanks for having me over, Mr. Morrow," Lizzy said.

"Always a pleasure, my dear!" His grin turned devilish as he rubbed his hands together. "Mwahaha, we'll see you on Friday to help set up the spooktacular party, right?"

"I wouldn't miss it for anything." Lizzy's blue eyes lit up.

"Ready, Lizzy?" Mr. Mackerville said. "Thanks again, Patrick."

"Not a problem. Have a safe trip." Mr. Morrow waved, then turned into the house.

Fairday hugged Lizzy goodbye, feeling her stomach twist in knots. It was one thing being brave with her friends around, but could she handle the next step on her own?

~ Twenty Three ~
THE PEN POINTS

Fairday climbed the spiral staircase and rounded the top. Her reflection gave an encouraging nod as she opened the door to DMS headquarters.

Settling down at the desk, she tapped a pencil to her chin. The energy in the room felt like the calm before a storm. So much had happened; everything needed to be kept straight. Her brain felt like a sponge, absorbing Ruby's clues as she wrote then in the notebook:

Magpie = bird - Edgar
- Told riddles/brought Ruby gifts - Thurston's pen
- Gave Ruby manifest of books
- Is this what Larry wants us to know?

Book collection - Ashpot Library - meet Larry Tuesday
Lizzy's picture of article
Odds are Thurston's treasures - the blue glass ball?
- Location is in a book - the secret's in Ruby's room
- Where is the secret hidden?

The last question stirred her thoughts. *Where did Ruby keep her secrets?* Feeling as ready as she'd ever be, Fairday flipped the notebook closed, stuck it in her backpack, and went to the wardrobe. Thank goodness this portal worked, and she didn't have to go through the mirror. It was the only way she felt remotely comfortable going to the other side alone. The mirror could be tricky. Knocking three times plus three, the claw handles unlatched. Fairday stepped over the blueprints, then knocked again. Cracking open the doors, she peeked out.

Fairday was back in Ruby's room. Dropping her pack on the red coverlet, she surveyed the scene. Everything was as they'd left it, still frozen in time. She felt alone, but was that true? Better to get started than worry. Crouching down, she checked under the bed, pushing the floorboards to see if any were loose. No such luck. Where to look next? Straightening up, an item on the dresser caught her eye, and she went over to investigate.

It was a black pen with a silver band. Could it be Thurston's? Ruby's words floated through her mind. Ink had the power to free thought, but could a pen point her in the right direction? Setting it down, her gaze moved over the perfume bottles. Fairday uncorked a pink one; the rosy smell conjured up images of her grandma's garden. She put it back, feeling weird about looking through Ruby's stuff. She *would not* want someone poking around her things, but she knew in this case, it had to be done.

The top drawer was crammed with papers. Keeping Ruby's privacy in mind, Fairday scanned through, looking for a connection to the Odds. Nothing popped out. She moved on to the next one. A glint of silver grabbed her attention. It was a pocket watch with a small inscription on the back. Fairday set it aside.

Her fingers began sifting and landed on a miniature model of the Eiffel Tower. She wondered what it meant to Ruby. Placing it by the watch, Fairday continued digging. The remaining contents revealed a compass, an origami crane, and a rabbit figurine. But what appeared to be the bottom of the drawer was actually a thin notepad.

Fairday lifted it out. Bingo! It was a list of books that were donated to the Ashpot Library. *The manifest that Edgar brought Ruby!* There were less than ten, but they all seemed to tie in with Eldrich: *Legends from the Black Forest, Ancient Hexes, Sands in Time, Book of Ends*— that fit, odds and ends? Yes! There it was, *Book of Odds.* Phew! Mission accomplished.

Fairday stuffed the manifest in her pack. After returning the other objects to the drawer, she glanced around one last time.

Tap. Tap. Tap. The sound came from outside the window.

Fairday froze. *What was that?*

Tap. Tap. Tap. Tap.

Her heart skipped. Was it the willow? Could it be Edgar? *Both were scary!*

Tap. Tap. Tap. Tap. Tap.

Whatever it was wanted in. Fairday had what she came for and could just go, but what if Fas was trying to reach her? Being brave was much easier with Lizzy and Marcus around! She went to the window and whipped back the drapes. Nothing to see. The willow tree swayed innocently and the ghosts mingled at the party. Business as usual in the backyard. Opening the stained glass window, Fairday leaned out to get a better look. *Whoosh!* A rush of black-and-white feathers flew in over her head.

"Whoa!" She ducked.

The bird landed on the dresser and flapped its wings.

"Hello," she said. It felt like she was in Ruby's story. *This must be Edgar!*

It turned a beady eye on her, then spoke. "A book-worm plots spinning line, catching words on which to dine. Look into the shadow's light, don't be tricked by wrong or right."

The bird hopped off the dresser, then flew out the window. Fairday slammed it shut, making sure the latch locked. Something shifted near the backpack. She picked it up by the straps, and shook the bag. Nothing there. Her mind must be frazzling! Fairday jotted the message in the notebook, along with the contents of the drawer. What was Edgar trying to tell her? Could the riddle be a warning? What would they find in the *Book of Odds*?

She had no idea, but the stakes were high and the plot was getting thicker.

ᴼᵛ Twenty Four ᵉᵛ
THE BUZZ AT BLOCK ROCK

Fairday clutched her backpack as the bus rumbled over a pothole on the way to school. Staring out the window, she listened absently to the Monday chatter. Most of the kids were talking about the earthquake that rattled the town.

"So, Fairday, are you excited for your party this weekend?"

"Sorry?" Fairday shook her daydream away.

Her classmate, Olivia, was turned in her seat, blonde hair bobbing to the rhythm of the bus. "I can't wait to see what your house looks like on the inside. It's so spooky!" Olivia glanced at her friends, their eyes now on Fairday.

"Yeah!" Fairday said. "Fear not the unexpected, ha ha." Her joke fell flat when everyone lurched forward as the bus pulled to a stop in front of Ashpot Elementary. Fairday gathered her things, then followed Olivia down the aisle. Stepping off, she saw Marcus and jogged over to him.

"Hi, Marcus."

"Hey, so what happened?"

"I have tons to tell you. I emailed Lizzy last night."

"We can talk at recess. Meetcha at Block Rock?"

"Sounds good." Fairday nodded as they walked into school.

A short, plump woman dressed in bright colors stood in front of the classroom, motioning for quiet. "Good morning, students. My name is Mrs. Honeyham, and I'll be teaching for Ms. Mason today. Please take out your math book and complete the review problems on page one oh three."

Snickers rippled through the room. Her name *was* a perfect fit. Fairday noticed that instead of being upset, Mrs. Honeyham smiled, not minding the humor.

The math assignment was easy and Fairday finished early. Staring at the clock, she willed it to move faster. Five minutes to go. Her eyes wandered. Marcus was bent over his work with a furrowed brow. Banner sat in front of him flicking the back of his seat.

Ding! Finally. Grabbing her stuff, Fairday slid into line. Waiting until recess to meet Marcus was torture, but at least now it was only a few hours away.

After lunch, they were led outside and kids ran off to play in groups. Walking across the field, Fairday turned toward a square mound jutting out of the grass, Block Rock.

Marcus waved when he saw her.

"Hi," Fairday said. "So a lot's happened." She slung off her pack and unzipped it.

"Excellent. Fill me in."

"We interviewed Ruby at Larry Lovell's house."

"And?"

"Well, she wasn't exactly thrilled to see us."

"Why not?"

Fairday lowered her voice. "Ruby thinks Eldrich is playing tricks again."

"She's probably right."

"I know. But all we have to go on is what Fas told us. I mean, it's hard to imagine what'll happen if the book-worm eats more words."

"I wonder what it looks like?" Marcus scratched his chin.

"I picture the bookworm with a top hat and monocle, eating sentences off a plate."

"Yeah, or like Cookie Monster, stuffing words into his mouth."

"Who knows? It could be a really smart person who eats books." Fairday grimaced.

"A human bookworm?" Marcus looked skeptical.

"AHHH!" someone behind them screamed.

Fairday and Marcus jumped and turned to see what had happened. A girl Fairday didn't know was waving her arms at them, hopping from foot to foot.

"What is it?" Fairday looked around, trying to find the source of the girl's terror.

"It was on your back!"

"What are you shouting about?" Marcus asked.

"THAT!" the girl yelled, pointing.

A huge brown spider was scurrying down the side of the rock. Fairday and Marcus shot each other a look. *Could it be Sanir?*

"Should I try to get him?" Fairday asked.

Marcus opened his mouth to answer, but was cut off.

"Catching spiders, Fairday?" Bart Monohan pushed aside the panicky girl. He rolled his eyes and made the crazy sign.

Fairday knew Bart wasn't a nice person; she'd witnessed his bad behavior before. The girl covered her eyes and ran away.

"Get lost, Bart," Marcus said and his jaw stiffened.

"Look, it's Brocket and Freakday, the happy couple," Bart said. He puckered his lips and made his round face look like a fish.

"I said, get lost." Marcus fixed his stare.

Fairday tensed. She didn't want there to be a fight!

"What's this?" Bart reached into Fairday's pack and whipped out the manifest.

"You're seriously going to regret that." Marcus stepped forward.

"Give it back, Bart," Dif said as he strode up to them. His buzzed hair and skull-and-crossbones jacket made him look intimidating. He stopped next to Bart and punched his fist.

"Whadda ya mean?" Bart sounded confused.

Fairday felt the same way, and judging by Marcus's dropped jaw, so did he. Dif was usually the ringleader of the mean kids.

"Just give it to her, dipwad," Dif said.

Bart looked unsure, then shrugged and handed the notepad to Fairday.

"Thanks," Fairday said.

Dif nodded and slapped Bart on the back as they headed across the field.

"Wow. Did that just happen? Dif must like you, Fairday."

136

"I invited him to my Halloween party."

"You did?" Marcus's eyes widened.

"Yep. Had to. Mom made me ask the whole class."

"Well, that had a positive outcome."

"As Lizzy would say, you betcha it did." Fairday beamed.

"So, what's that?" Marcus gestured to the manifest.

"A clue."

Marcus's eyes scanned the titles. "What's it mean?"

"Well first, we found out that Ruby had a pet bird named Edgar that gave her things."

"Like what?"

"All sorts of stuff, but one thing is important. Ruby said Edgar recently showed up at Larry's house and told her a riddle."

"Really? What'd he say?"

"Edgar said for her to tell us where the Odds are."

"You mean like numbers?"

"No, Odds are what Thurston called his treasures."

Marcus's expression was blank, then, like a light bulb turned on in his head, he exclaimed, "The blue glass ball! Maybe I didn't break it!"

"Right. Their location is written in a book that was donated to the Ashpot Library. Edgar gave Ruby *this* manifest of Thurston's book collection before I moved in. I found it last night."

"Holy cow. What—" Marcus stopped talking when the bell rang. "Dang. I've gotta run. I told Banner I'd meet him in line before class. Pick this up later?"

"Okay," Fairday said. Banner was Marcus's best friend and the class clown. She didn't know him very well yet, but he did seem funny.

On their way back, Marcus jogged ahead and Fairday lagged behind, keeping an eye out for the spider. Was it Sanir? Why would he hitch a ride with her to school? The day was turning out to be full of surprises, and Fairday had a feeling there were more to come.

~e Twenty Five e~
LESSON LEARNED

Mrs. Honeyham called everyone to the back of the room. "Please join me on the carpet. Bring your copy of *Charlotte's Web* if you'd like to follow along." Kids found their usual spots, some with books, others choosing to listen. Fairday's thoughts were spinning. Was Sanir creeping around her school as a spider? If so, she didn't think it'd lead to anything good.

When the chattering ceased, Mrs. Honeyham said, "Today we're going to pay close attention to the way the author gets the characters' feelings across. We'll be talking about this during our mini lesson. Ready then? 'Chapter One: Before Breakfast.'"

Fairday closed her eyes. Like magic, she was transported to the farm with Fern and the barn animals. Her imagination drifted through the scenes, absorbing them. Then came the part that always made her cringe—when Mr. Arable explains that it's more humane to kill the runt pig, and Fern cannot believe how unfair he's being. Fairday felt Fern's fury rise when Mr. Arable tells her to control herself—*wait, what?*

Fairday's ears pricked up. The passage Mrs. Honeyham read was wrong. Glancing at the book in her lap, she saw an important word missing, just like in her copy of *The Wizard of Oz*! Instead of Mr. Arable telling Fern to control herself, it read, "You will have to learn to yourself." The response, "'Myself?' Fern yelled. 'This is a matter of life and death, and you talk about myself.'" Without control and controlling, the story had changed.

A chill crept up her spine as Mrs. Honeyham continued on, not skipping a beat. The words were gone, as if they'd never been there at all. *No one even noticed!* If Fairday didn't know the story by heart, she wasn't sure if she'd have caught it. Was this the work of the bookworm? Or only misprinted copies? Fairday had to get to the bottom of it. If the bookworm *was* the culprit, it seemed her most beloved stories were the soup du jour.

Mrs. Honeyham closed the book. "When you get back to your seats, take out your writer's notebook and jot down what you've learned about the characters so far."

Fairday got right to work, but her nerves were on edge, and when she pressed the pencil tip to the paper, it broke. Crossing the room toward the sharpener, she glanced at Marcus, certain he wasn't aware anything was amiss.

The pencil vibrated to the electric buzz and Fairday looked out the window. As her eyes adjusted to the sunlight, she gasped. The words LOST CONTROL were woven into a silvery web that glinted from the top corner. *It had to be a message from Sanir!* She checked around for the spider, trying not to be obvious. If anyone else caught sight of him, it would be chaos in the classroom—a lot worse than one frightened girl.

"Young lady, I think your pencil's had enough."

Fairday jumped. "Sorry? Oh!" she said, realizing she'd sharpened it to a nub. All eyes were on her. Hoping no one saw the web, she hurried back to her seat. Once at her desk, Fairday caught Marcus's eye and pointed to the window. He turned, his gaze following her finger, then snapped his head back, eyes big as saucers.

Fairday tapped her wrist; their secret signal to meet up in the hallway. Marcus winked, then bent over his

141

desk. She finished up her work, which wasn't easy with the nub. Plus it was hard to know what to write—the characters' feelings had changed.

An idea popped into her head, and Fairday saw an opportunity to do a little investigating. Walking over to Mrs. Honeyham, she asked if she could go to the library to check out a book. Luckily, the answer was yes, and Fairday left the room.

A moment later Marcus appeared in the hallway with the bathroom pass. "So, what's with the web?"

"It has to be Sanir," Fairday whispered.

"Yeah, but why's he here?"

"No idea. Maybe someone's trying to kidnap him too. Who knows what's going on in the Talking Library with Fas gone."

"Hopefully, Alice isn't in charge." Marcus rolled his eyes.

"Or the Shadow Rook." Fairday frowned.

"What do you think the message means?"

"I'm not sure, but during read aloud, I noticed that the word control was gone from a passage in *Charlotte's Web*." Fairday twisted her ponytail. "Which is why I'm headed to the library. If the school's copy is missing words, then the bookworm's feasting."

"Good idea. Then what?"

"I'm meeting Larry Lovell at the Ashpot Library to-morrow. Hopefully, he can help find the *Book of Odds* in Thurston's private collection, and then we can figure out how to call Eldrich."

"What should we do about Sanir?"

"What *can* we do? If we're lucky, he'll stay out of sight."

Marcus nodded, giving a thumbs up as he disappeared into the classroom. Fairday walked down the hall and swung open the door to the library.

The assistant smiled as she approached. "Hello, Fair-day. Can I help you?"

"Hi, Mr. Peterson. I'm checking out a book."

"You're in the right place then," he said and gestured to the rows of shelves.

Fairday went to find *Charlotte's Web*. Flipping to chapter one, she scanned the passage; her heart sank. The words were gone. The bookworm was probably licking its inky chops!

On her way out, Fairday spotted another web over the exit sign, STOP WORM spun into it. Sanir definitely wanted her attention! Squaring her shoulders, Fairday left the library. That's exactly what she intended to do!

That evil bookworm was toast, and *she* ate toast for breakfast.

⌒ Twenty Six ⌒
A PRIVATE COLLECTION

The Morrow family cruiser sped toward the Ashpot Library, twisting along country roads. Margo was asleep in her car seat, and Fairday watched out the window while her dad hummed to the tune on the radio.

"There's Mr. Lovell," he said as they pulled up to the curb.

Larry Lovell was by the library door, tapping his cane with one hand and frowning at his watch on his other arm.

"Thanks for bringing me, Dad." Fairday stepped out of the car and grabbed her backpack.

Mr. Morrow leaned over the seat. "Happy to help! Now, you have the phone, so call when you're ready to be picked up. Did you remember the books Mr. Lovell asked you to bring?"

"Yep. Got 'em here." Fairday patted the bag. She knew that part was a ruse, but had it covered just in case. Mr. Morrow honked and wove into traffic. Fairday walked up the steps.

"Miss Morrow." Larry tipped his hat.

"Hi," Fairday answered, not sure what to say just yet.

Larry cleared his throat. "Hm, mm. Well, we've plenty to discuss, but first let's get out of this cold." He opened the door, and they went into the library.

Larry must've set things up ahead of time, because once the librarian noticed him, she waved, bustling around the desk to greet them.

Grasping his hand, she said, "Nice to see you. I've only a moment, so I'll take you down to private collections now."

Fairday wasn't sure what Larry was after, but they seemed to be on the same path.

"Hello, Joan. Appreciate your time. Hm, mm. I'm helping this young lady here with a project, and there's no better place to get a clue than the library."

Joan smiled her approval. Nodding at Fairday, she said, "Well, dear, there's no one better to help you with research. Mr. Lovell's quite a famous investigative jour-nalist, you know?"

Fairday started to answer, but Joan didn't wait for a response; instead she turned, knit sweater swishing, as she gestured for them to follow her downstairs. The steps led to a hall with book covers painted along the walls, names of donors written in black. A short way down they stopped at a door: **PRIVATE COLLECTIONS**.

Fishing the key ring out of her pocket, Joan unlocked the room, then shuffled them in. "Now, Mr. Lovell knows the rules, but it's my duty to remind you. Gloves must be worn, and there's no flash photography. It goes without saying, nothing leaves this area."

Fairday felt a tingle touch her spine as she walked in. Long glass cases filled with objects lined the walls, and a balcony wrapped around, revealing an upper level with aisles of bookshelves. How many mysteries lived here? She could spend ages investigating and never solve them all. Crossing her fingers, she hoped the odds would be in her favor.

Joan pointed to tables in the center of the room. "Normally, we have someone sit with patrons using the archives, but as there's no one who's used them more than you, Larry, I'll leave you to your business. Call from the wall phone if you need anything."

147

"Thanks, Joan. I know what's what," Larry grumbled, then hung his cane on a chair.

Fairday dropped her backpack and gave the librarian a reassuring nod.

"Well, it looks like everything's in order." Joan clapped her hands. "Good luck with your project!" She closed the door on her way out.

Larry eyed Fairday behind wire-rim glasses. "Do you know why we're here?"

"Is it because of what Edgar told Ruby?"

"Yes, but there's more to it. I have a hunch Richard Bittner's involved."

Fairday was about to ask who Richard Bittner was, but Larry's eyes shifted. "Hm, mm, let's not get ahead of ourselves. First things first, we work with what we know." Turning, he went to the computer at the end of the table.

Fairday followed and pulled up a chair, pen ready to jot down their findings.

"We can uncover the answers we seek, if we search the right words." Larry wiggled his fingers over the keyboard. "Simple phrases are best. Begonia, private collection." Within seconds the catalog displayed: Section E5, 1st floor.

Larry tipped his glasses to the end of his nose and turned to Fairday. "There's our starting point. Let's see what we've got."

Putting on gloves, they walked toward a plaque on the wall with E5 engraved on it. All sorts of objects rested on a blue velvet background. A bronze nameplate with Begonia popped out from the display, and Fairday leaned in to get a better look. There was a glass-blown flute with a rose painted on the mouthpiece; next to it was a wooden jewelry box. Both were interesting and beautiful, but neither was what she was looking for.

"See anything of interest?" Larry asked.

"I'm pretty sure the answers I need are in a book."

"Hm, mm, you're hot on the trail then." Larry pointed to the cabinets under the exhibit. "That's where books pertaining to Thurston's collection are kept."

Fairday knelt down and pulled the brass knobs. Scanning the sideways titles, her heart jumped when she recognized them from the manifest. *This had to be right!* She ticked them off in her head: *Ancient Hexes, Sands in Time, Legends from the Black Forest,* but wait, the *Book of Ends* wasn't there. Were there missing volumes? With a silent wish, she read the last spine on the shelf: the

Book of Odds. It was here! A piece of the puzzle just fell into place.

Holding her breath, Fairday pulled out the worn leather journal. The book smelled of magic—a touch of sage, with hints of eucalyptus and lavender. The edges were gold and the pages felt like tissue paper. Very carefully, she turned them. Each entry had a picture and description. Flipping through, she stopped on an image of a blue ball. Could that be the one they were looking for? It seemed similar to the trinket Marcus had broken, but the only way to know for sure was to find it.

"What've you got there?" Larry asked, peering over her shoulder.

Fairday's tongue was stuck. Should she tell him the whole story? Larry *knew* something or they wouldn't be here; plus he'd helped the DMS solve their last case.

Fairday set the journal down and took out her phone. "The manifest Ruby got from Edgar included a list of Thurston's books. This was on it." Turning off the flash, she snapped pictures, zooming in on the pages. "In our last case, we found a letter from Thurston that described a way to contact Eldrich. We think there's a clue in here that'll lead us to it."

Larry's eyebrows raised. "So *you are* trying to contact Eldrich? Ruby feared that's what you kids were up to. She sounds like a dangerous character to get involved with. Do you think it's wise, Miss Morrow?"

Taking a deep breath, Fairday filled him in on what had been happening with the bookworm and the Talking Library. As crazy as it all sounded, Larry listened and gave no reaction other than nodding. Fairday felt comfortable talking to him, thinking he must've been a good journalist. She started explaining about the missing words when he snapped his fingers.

"I knew it! Richard Bittner *must* be involved."

"Who's Richard Bittner?"

"Bittner writes for the *Ashpot Weekly*, and he's known for mincing words in his reports. He said some strange things in his article about this collection. He always messes up the news, but this was different. I started to pay closer attention, knowing in my gut there was more to the story." Larry paused, scratching his chin. "Then, when Ruby told me about Edgar, I felt certain I was right. That snake of a reporter's up to something, and I plan to find out what it is."

"So you think Edgar's visit to Ruby is connected to Richard Bittner's article about this collection?" Fairday's eyes grew wide. Was it possible that a local reporter was working for the bookworm? That seemed unlikely, but so had everything in this case.

"I'm not certain, but my instincts say they are."

Fairday placed the *Book of Odds* back on the shelf and took pictures of all the books in the cabinet. Standing up, she asked, "What's wrong with his story?"

"The only thing that *can* be wrong with a news report—it isn't true. Bittner manipulated his words to serve an agenda. He's always got one. Sometimes it takes awhile to see what angle he's coming from. He's got people fooled, but not me. I won't be surprised if he *is* in cahoots with that bookworm. I'd love to see what the folks in Ashpot say then."

Fairday couldn't imagine what would happen if everyone in town found out about the secrets the Begonia House was hiding. Would they want to destroy it? *That* would be terrible!

Larry picked up his cane and Fairday slung her pack on. Walking out, he turned to her. "Hm, mm. I understand your reasoning for calling Eldrich, but I would advise caution. Ruby lost half her life because she was hoodwinked by that trickster."

"Fas warned us about her too, but he also said if we don't succeed, words will be lost and stories will change. *That* cannot happen." Fairday felt the force behind her words.

"You must do what you think is right, but remember to consider *all* angles. Just as shadows are revealed by light, truth lies betwixt the lines."

"Thanks, Mr. Lovell," Fairday said as they left the room. Larry's words reminded her of something Edgar had said about the shadow's light. She couldn't remember the exact phrase; good thing it was written in her notebook!

This case was heating up, and with her Halloween party on the horizon, Fairday had no idea how things would unfold. Finding the *Book of Odds* felt like a step forward, but in which direction? If they did *actually* manage to contact Eldrich, what then? One thing was for sure, Fairday wanted to be prepared, and that meant teamwork!

~ Twenty Seven ~
MISSING PIECES

After dinner that night, the kitchen was quiet. Everyone had taken to their own activities in other parts of the house. Auntie Em was snoozing on her cushion in the corner. Fairday took the laptop off the counter and brought it to the table. Logging in, she pulled up her email and clicked open a new message from Lizzy.

F -

enlarged pic of article from larry's house - not sure why he has it hung up - some guy named richard bittner wrote it. i googled him and he's a reporter for the ashpot weekly newspaper. it's not written very well, also he's got some of his facts wrong. the date of the article and what ruby said in her interview don't match up. also, some bizarre news - i overheard aunt forsey talking about a german ancestor who had magic shoes!!! what could that mean?

what happened at the library w/ larry? did you find the book of odds? any more webs with messages? we have tons to figure out! can't wait for your party this weekend! mom's dropping me off after school friday. my costume's all set. gotta run, homework to do!!!
ttyl ~ L

Fairday hit reply and began to type. The keys clicked to her thoughts, and they flowed onto the screen. She didn't worry about the formalities with Lizzy and wrote in a relaxed style. Time was flying and the puzzle was getting more complicated. There were still so many missing pieces! Thank goodness Lizzy would be here soon to help put the clues in order.

L-
what you found out about the article goes with what i learned at the library. larry thinks richard bittner could be involved with the bookworm - more to tell you about this. btw! i found thurston's collection and it was missing a book. luckily that one was called the book of ends, but i found the book of odds! in it there's a picture that looks like the blue glass ball! omg though - are we really going to call eldrich if we

find it? larry doesn't think it's a good idea. idk, we have to, right? crazy about the magic shoes!!! can't wait to hear the story.

no webs or signs of sanir since yesterday at school - idk where he is? excited about the party, but worried the case won't be solved in time. yikes!
ttyl ~F

Fairday shut down the computer. Auntie Em let out a snore and lazily scratched her ear. With nothing left that could be done to make progress, Fairday decided to call it a night.

Without warning, Auntie Em leaped up, bounding out of the kitchen, barking like mad. Fairday peeked out into the foyer just as the doorbell rang.

Mr. Morrow approached the door before Fairday got there and put an eye to the peephole. "Who is it?"

No answer.

He opened the door.

Nobody was there, only leaves blowing across the porch.

Shrugging, he shut it, then patted the pug's head. "Okay, calm down, old girl. Doorbell's probably broken." Auntie

Em sneezed, waddling after him into the parlor.

Fairday hoped her dad was right. Otherwise, someone was playing a joke, and she *did not* think it was funny. Teeth on edge, she climbed the stairs to her room.

Now that the window was fixed, Fairday was in her own space. She lay back on the pillow and let her mind relax. Her wandering eyes fell upon a mark on the bedpost and she sat up to get a better look. A crown was carved into the wood. Fairday ran her finger over it, wondering what the symbol meant and whose bed it was before. It seemed everything that had been left behind in the Begonia House had a story to tell. Settling into her covers, Fairday closed her eyes. Despite racing thoughts, sleep came, and she sank into a dream.

Twenty Eight
A WAYWARD WARNING

Fairday twisted her ponytail, waiting for the pictures she'd taken at the library to print. The last image slid out, and she picked up the stack. The top one was the first page in the *Book of Odds,* which had a handwritten verse: *Find the Odds with even eyes. Lines reveal truth in lies. Not by magic will you see. Nursery rhymes are the key.*

Thurston must've written this inscription. It sounded like *not* using magic was the way to uncover his treasures. But how were nursery rhymes involved? Fairday had grown up reading Mother Goose, which had inspired her love of riddles. She hoped knowing the stories would help solve the case. Slipping the pictures into a folder, Fairday turned to go. Suddenly, she froze. Something was scratching at the door across the hall.

"Auauuuuuu," Auntie Em howled from the other side.

"Oh my gosh!" Fairday ran and swung open the door. How did Auntie Em get trapped? That room was always closed! With all the work to do downstairs, it was still set up as Thurston Begonia's study, and she hadn't even been in there since the last case.

The little pug raced out, scampering down the stairs. Fairday walked in to check it out. The velvet drapes were drawn, giving the space a hazy green glow. Her eyes adjusted to the dim light and she saw something on the floor. It was her leather-bound edition of *Harry Potter and the Sorcerer's Stone*! *WHAT? How did it get in here?* That book should be with *her* private collection in her room. Heart racing, she snatched it up and saw a piece of paper sticking out.

Opening the book, Fairday took out the note and glanced at the page it marked: "Chapter Three: The Letters from No One." A flashback of leaves blowing across her front porch gave her goose bumps. No one was there when her dad had answered the door. *Coincidence?*

Looking at the note, the first strange thing Fairday spotted was that it was typed, and the lines were messed up. The other was that it *didn't* rhyme, while all the others had.

**Get the
scoop.
stop hunt
or
the next course will be
spells.**

Fairday didn't think this message was from Sanir. Did the bookworm send it? Or somebody else? Was a stranger creeping around her house? From past experience, she knew it was more likely than not! Checking her nerves, Fairday reread the words.

Get the scoop made her think of the news, but course *could* mean meal. It seemed like the message implied that if they didn't stop looking for the Odds, the next plate in the bookworm's feast would be spells from Harry Potter. Oh. Double. Oh no. That really hurt, but she couldn't give up! There was too much at stake. Lizzy was *not* going to be happy about this.

Ding, dong! The doorbell rang, echoing through the house.

Fairday jumped. Who could it be now?

Creeping to the end of the hall, she peeked down the stairs. Her mom answered the door; someone *was* there this time. A short man wearing a baseball cap with a camera strapped around his neck stood on the porch with a ready handshake.

"Evening, ma'am. I'm Richard Bittner, reporter with the *Ashpot Weekly*. I'd, uh, like to ask you some questions about the business you plan to open here."

Richard Bittner was at her house! He didn't look or sound very professional. She could see why Larry didn't like him.

"Oh my! How exciting." Her mom sounded delighted. "Won't you please come in?"

"Thank ya." His eyes shifted as he slunk in. He removed his cap and ran a hand over his forehead. "Interesting place you, uh, got here, lots of stories about it."

"So I've heard!" Mrs. Morrow answered. "With my interior design business and the renovations, I'm afraid I'm too busy right now to talk. But an appointment I had scheduled for Friday evening cancelled, and I'm free at seven, if you'd like to stop by then. The grand opening of the bed and breakfast won't be for a while, though I'd love to get a buzz going."

"Well, I can, uh, help you there," Bittner said, pointing his camera and snapping a shot. "That's the plan. See you Friday night." He pulled his cap down and flicked his tongue before turning to go.

"Thank you! Goodbye." Mrs. Morrow waved, shutting the door. With a skip in her step, she headed into the kitchen. "Pat, you'll never guess who that was —"

Fairday could not believe it. Richard Bittner would be here Friday night! She and Lizzy had their work cut out for them. *Was* the reporter working for the bookworm? It seemed strange that he showed up right when she found the note. Holy cow! Maybe Bittner was the messenger this time. She shuddered at the thought of him lurking around her house.

Back in her room, Fairday set the folder with the pictures on top of her DMS pack. Everything was ready to roll for Lizzy's visit. Sitting on the bed, she pulled out her math homework. Numbers were no problem. Fairday had a feeling it was the upcoming weekend that would really put her skills to the test.

~ Twenty Nine ~
WALL SPIES

Lights in DMS headquarters were blazing Friday evening. Lizzy had finally arrived, and Fairday filled her in about the unexpected visitor and upcoming interview.

"Oh my gosh! Weird that Richard Bittner showed up here. Do you really think he's involved with the Talking Library?"

"It's possible. The bookworm and Bittner are both after words. One's eating them and the other's messing them up." Fairday uncorked the blueprints, unrolling the sheets on the carpet. "I think these'll help us eavesdrop on the conversation tonight."

"Brilliant idea!" Lizzy exclaimed, kneeling down for a closer look.

Fairday pulled out a page and pointed to a phrase. "I found this earlier."

Lizzy leaned in and read aloud, *"When you want to listen in, ask the walls to begin. Tap them once, tap them twice, speak the room out on the thrice."* She glanced at Fairday. "So we tap the walls three times, then say the room we want to spy on? What happens next?"

"No clue. We should try it first."

"You betcha!" Lizzy jumped up. "Who's in the parlor now?"

"I think my dad's watching his cooking show in there."

"Perfect!" Lizzy tucked her still limp hair behind her ear. Nodding at Fairday, she faced the wall. *Tap.* pause. *Tap.* pause. On the third tap, she said, "Parlor room!"

The wall rippled and began to fade, then it appeared as a blank screen.

"Okay. Now what?" Lizzy asked, shrugging.

The wall clicked on like a TV, only this channel was her dad in his "Got Food" apron, watching a blender mash fruit. When the host poured green juice over a red cake, Mr. Morrow yelled, "NO!" The sound came in crisp and clear.

Their plan had worked! Lizzy and Fairday grinned at each other.

"Too bad Marcus isn't here. He'd love this feature." Lizzy touched the wall. "So how do we turn it off?"

Fairday scanned the blueprints. "Here's the answer! *Walls are spies with no eyes. To let them rest, sing your best.*"

"Eh?" Lizzy tilted her head.

"I think you have to sing." Fairday looked up at her partner.

"Hope my *best* is good enough!" Lizzy threw back her head and belted out, "Happy birthday to you."

The screen went black and the crumbling wallpaper returned. Now they had front row seats to Bittner's interview. It felt good to have a few tricks up *their* sleeves.

The next item on the agenda was to work out the clues from the *Book of Odds*. Finding the blue glass ball was their best chance at beating the bookworm. The only other option was to use the high-heeled sneakers, but it could take ages to figure out how that magic worked.

Fairday spread out the pictures she'd printed. The writing around the ball was hard to see, so she'd blown up the images to read the descriptions better.

Lizzy picked one up. "This line says, 'Fighting for the crown.'"

Fairday jolted upright. "Lizzy! I forgot to tell you. Yesterday I found a crown symbol carved into my bedpost."

"That might tie in somehow!" Lizzy grabbed another. "'All around the town.'"

"I hope that doesn't mean the Odds are scattered in Ashpot," Fairday said, reaching into the pile. "Here's a weird one, 'Some gave them plum-cake.'"

"Hm. Maybe they're in the kitchen?"

Fairday looked over the stack of sentences. They sounded familiar. Lion caught her attention and she read the line. Spotting unicorn, she snapped her fingers. "I've got it!"

Fairday arranged the photos so the text read:

The Lion and the Unicorn

were fighting for the crown,

The Lion beat the Unicorn

all around the town.

Some gave them white bread,

and some gave them brown,

Some gave them plum-cake,

and sent them out of town.

"It's a nursery rhyme!" Fairday beamed.

"I never would've gotten that. See, Wordcaster, I knew your skills would come in handy." Lizzy patted her back.

"The carpet in my room has a lion and a unicorn. Maybe the Odds are hidden under it?"

"That theory fits! Let's find out if you're right!" Lizzy grabbed her DMS pack.

"Should we call Eldrich if we find the blue glass ball?"

"We'll have to think about it. Let's just see if it's even there." Lizzy turned to leave.

Winding down the spiral staircase, Fairday wondered if her instincts were right. But was calling Eldrich a good idea? Gathering her wits, she stepped further into the mystery.

❧

~ Thirty ~
LIES BENEATH

Fairday grabbed one corner of the carpet, Lizzy the other. The girls heaved the thick rug to the side. Just like the lion and unicorn fighting in the scene, the struggle was real.

"Oh my gosh! There's a trapdoor in the floor!" Fairday exclaimed, pointing.

"I don't see a handle though."

"Me neither? Wonder how it opens?"

"Hm. Let's see." Lizzy took the headlamp out of her pack. Strapping on the gear, she said, "Time for a closer inspection."

Fairday grabbed her magnifying glass and inched around the door. She pressed on it, but the wood didn't budge. Fairday thought for a moment, then stood and walked over to the post. *Could the crown symbol have something to do with it?* She pushed, then rubbed the etching. Nothing.

"I'm stumped!" Lizzy said. She sat on her knees and blew a puff of hair.

169

"The nursery rhyme might be the key to finding the Odds, but I can't guess how it'll get us in. Thurston wrote that magic won't help, and I don't think we can pry this open."

"We'll have to work on it later. Let's get back to headquarters before Bittner meets your mom." Lizzy stood up.

Headlights flashed through the window. It had to be about seven. Richard Bittner was here. The interview was going to start!

Fairday and Lizzy sat on the floor, notepads ready. Eyes on the wall, they saw Mrs. Morrow usher the reporter into the parlor.

"He *does* remind me of a worm." Lizzy observed.

"Wait until you hear his voice," Fairday said.

Bittner slunk in through the door, sneakers squeaking as he poked around the room.

"Please, have a seat." Mrs. Morrow gestured to the couch, then sat in the opposite chair. "I'm excited to tell you all the wonderful plans we have for this glorious Queen Anne Victorian. My husband, Pat, can't join us; our two-year-old was having a bit of a tantrum, and he's getting her ready for bed."

Bittner continued to wander, picking up a picture frame, then setting it down.

Mrs. Morrow tried to get his attention. "It might be easier to talk if you sit. I'm sure you have lots of questions about the renovations."

"Yes, ma'am." Bittner strode over, camera swinging around his neck. Pushing the brim of his baseball cap, he ran a hand across his forehead. "Can't wait to, uh, hear."

"Where would you like to start?" Mrs. Morrow folded her hands in her lap, playing with her wedding ring.

Fairday knew her mom only did that when she felt uncomfortable.

Bittner flopped on the couch and opened his notebook. He pulled out a pen and leaned forward. "How'd the old place hold up through the, uh, earthquake?"

Fairday felt a shiver. "That's a weird question."

"It is, but it *could* fit with his story." Lizzy jotted down a note.

"I guess." Fairday did not think Bittner was here to write about renovations.

Mrs. Morrow straightened her skirt and shifted position. "Just fine. Minor bumps and bruises, but nothing we can't fix. My husband always says, 'Problems are possibilities.'"

From their vantage point, they could see what Bittner was writing in his notebook. It was just squiggly lines, no words. *He was faking it!*

"No, uh, major damage then. Didn't stir up any ghosts?"

The edges of Mrs. Morrow's mouth turned down. Never a good sign. "Not that I'm aware of." Reaching for a folder, she changed the conversation. "Here's an outline of the improvements we're working on." Passing it across the table, she forced a smile.

"Thank ya. I'll check this, uh, later." Bittner tossed the folder aside. "So, no misfortunes, no ghosts. Where's the, uh, charm?" He flicked his tongue.

"Well, Mr. Bittner, the *charm* is building a dream with my family. This house has a legacy, and now we're a part of it. I plan to make my mark."

"Really? I'm sure folks in Ashpot will, uh, appreciate that." Bittner scribbled, then flipped the notebook closed. Standing, he snapped some photos, none of Mrs. Morrow.

Fairday could sense her mom's distress. The interview was *not* going well.

"Alrighty, then. I've got the, uh, story I came for." He tugged his baseball cap. Bittner spun on his heels, then left the room before Mrs. Morrow could show him out. She started to rise from the chair, her mouth open. But the door slammed, and he was gone.

"Your turn to get rid of the TV." Lizzy smiled at Fairday.

"Eh, em." Fairday cleared her throat, then sang, "I'm a little teapot, short and stout."

The wall returned and the girls looked at each other. Fairday knew in her gut Larry was right—Bittner was up to no good. But *why* was he snooping around her house?

"That reporter seems shady. He didn't ask any real questions," Lizzy said.

"Yeah, for sure. My mom *was not* happy." Fairday shook her head.

"Why do you think he wants to know about the earthquake?"

"No idea, but it's more evidence that he's involved with the bookworm."

Packing up, the two girls gathered the clues and rolled up the blueprints. Fairday knocked on the wardrobe and placed everything inside for safekeeping. Tomorrow was the big day—the Halloween extravaganza. Not figuring out how to open the trapdoor was a major setback. Luckily, Marcus would be there in the morning, and they'd have a few hours to work on the case before guests arrived for the party.

ᷲᷣ Thirty One ᷣᷲ
TWISTS AND TURNS

Saturday morning, Mr. Morrow whipped up a breakfast of omelets, fresh bread, and raspberries, perfect fuel for their bookworm hunt. The next step was to get the Odds, but where would they find a key to a door with no lock? Fairday didn't know. Bittner's visit *was* suspicious, and she felt certain there were more forces at work, but whose side were they on?

The doorbell rang. It was ten o'clock. Marcus had arrived.

Mr. Morrow peeped through the eyehole. "I don't think it's a vampire. Goblin perhaps."

"Dad, answer the door." Fairday smirked.

Mr. Morrow swung open the double doors. "Mwa-haha! Who goes there?"

Fairday rolled her eyes. Her dad was serious about the spooktacularness of the event.

"Hey, Mr. Morrow." Marcus shifted a bulging bag and his backpack.

"Provisions?" Mr. Morrow raised an eyebrow.

"Yeah, I brought my costume for tonight, so I don't have to go home."

"Smart man, knows how to manage time." He stepped aside.

"Hey." Marcus nodded at Fairday and Lizzy.

"Hi," they replied in unison.

Marcus strode over to them, lugging the bags.

Mr. Morrow clapped his hands. "Now, Detective Mystery Squad, I'm sure you're hot on the heels of some mystery or another. Why don't you get cracking on your case? I plan to conjure up the Halloween spirits around here." Pulling his shirt collar, he shifted his eyes. *Tonight!* Under the cloak of darkness, all shall be revealed." With a straight face, he added, "But not till then, so off with you! Fairday, here." He gave her the cell phone. "Mom and I will be all over this place since Margo's with Grandma, call if you need us."

"Thanks, Dad." Fairday took the phone.

"See you later, kiddos. Have fun," Mr. Morrow said and headed back to the kitchen.

The three detectives climbed the stairs. The partygoers were coming at five and the clock was ticking. Fairday had no clue how long it took a bookworm to eat words in stories, but she did know there was no time to waste. The DMS was on the case to save the books!

Once in Fairday's bedroom, the girls filled Marcus in about Bittner's interview, showed him the trapdoor, and pointed out the crown on the bedpost.

Marcus went through the same routine, then tried to get the door open. "This symbol seems like it means something." He traced the carving on the bedpost with his finger.

"I know, right? Maybe it does, but we couldn't figure it out," Lizzy said.

Marcus rubbed his chin. "I think we need to release a lever under the floor that will pop the lid. Maybe there's another spot to push that will create a chain reaction."

They scattered and searched for a button, or something similar. Nothing seemed like it would do the trick. Marcus walked back over to the bedpost.

"Not ready to give up on that yet, eh?" Lizzy asked.

"Nope. It's here for a reason, plus it goes with the nursery rhyme." He shook the post, then twisted it. Suddenly, something happened. It sounded like a gear turned under the bed.

"What'd you do?" Lizzy asked, eyes wide.

"Just turned it."

Without warning, there was a click and the wood popped up a crack.

"Excellent work, Marcus. You figured it out!" Fairday said.

"You betcha! Serious sleuthing skills, Brocket." Lizzy applauded.

"You don't have to tell me twice." Marcus winked and raised the door.

～ Thirty Two ～
A TRICKY CALL

Fairday, Lizzy, and Marcus lay flat on the floor of Fairday's bedroom and stared into the hole. Lizzy's headlamp lit up a cramped room and shadows outlined objects on shelves. *The Odds!* This had to be right.

"I see the bottom." Marcus jumped into the hole.

"Marcus!" Lizzy threw out her arms.

"What?" He looked up from a few feet below.

"Nothing." She blushed.

"What do you see?" Fairday asked.

Lizzy swiveled her head, and Marcus glanced around. From what Fairday could tell, there were a couple dozen items. She noticed a stone pestle and mortar next to a costume mask.

Marcus picked something up.

"What's that?" Fairday asked.

"A key with a note. Too dark to read in here."

"Send it up."

Marcus passed it to Fairday. The key was similar to the one that unlocked the front gates of the Begonia

House, only the note read: *Master's Emporium*. What could that be?

"Hey! I think I found it!" He knelt to pick an item off the bottom shelf.

"Nice work, Brocket. Let's see." Lizzy held out her hand and took the glass ball.

It was just like the one in Thurston's book! The glass ball Marcus had broken was much smaller. This one looked like a crystal ball, only it was deep blue, like the ocean.

Marcus pulled himself out like a pro, then faced the girls.

"Let's get back to HQ. It's time to call Eldrich," Fairday said.

"You betcha!" Lizzy tucked her hair behind her ears.

"Let's do this thing." Marcus gave them a thumbs up. They pulled the rug back in place and grabbed their gear, ready for the next step.

Back in DMS headquarters, the detectives sat around the blue glass ball, discussing their options. They needed to think it out carefully before they made the call.

"We need to remember that Fas said Eldrich is neither good or bad," Lizzy said.

"Yeah, but also that she's only out for herself." Fairday bit her thumbnail. "Eldrich might trick us, or help us. It depends whose side she's on. Fas needs her magic to stop the bookworm. We'll have to be careful."

"Eh, em," Marcus interrupted. "Excuse me, but we should talk about how we're going to get her to the Talking Library."

Lizzy puffed her hair. "He's right. Supposedly, an opportunity will present itself."

"Well, then"—Fairday shrugged—"I guess that's the answer. We'll just have to see what happens. "

"So who's going to do it?" Marcus asked.

"I will." Lizzy unzipped her pack and took out the high-heeled sneakers. She slipped them on. "These might protect me from her spells."

"Plus maybe like in *The Wizard of Oz* you have to be wearing them or Eldrich can take them back," Fairday said.

Lizzy nodded, then grasped the ball and called, "Eldrich."

~ Thirty Three ~
EVEN THE ODDS

Fairday didn't breathe, and for a moment, nothing happened. Then it looked like a swarm of black dots were moving through the center of the glass orb.

"What's happening?" Lizzy asked as it floated into the air.

The globe expanded above their heads, and Fairday saw the shadow of a woman approaching, getting larger as it came closer. The glass popped, like a bubble, and then she was there with them. The blue ball rematerialized on the floor, intact.

Silence enveloped the room as the DMS faced Eldrich. There was a glow around her, but the weirdest part was that she had the same round face and springy blonde hair as Lizzy. Before the Shadow Rook had taken her curls out anyway.

Fairday was certain Eldrich was powerful. After all, she'd just arrived through a glass ball. That must take some serious skills! Fairday could feel a frenzy of butterflies in her stomach.

Eldrich spun on heeled boots, considering each of them. She turned to Lizzy and pointed at the shoes. "I see my magic's born in thee, a relative you must be!" Her voice had a tinkling quality to it. She wasn't at all like the hag Ruby made her out to be. Was this a trick?

Lizzy's face was blank, and Fairday could tell her friend was experiencing mixed emotions. After all, she'd recently found out an ancestor may have had magical shoes. Could it be true? Was Lizzy related to a Myxtress?

Eldrich frowned and stepped up to Lizzy, examining her from inches away.

Lizzy stood her ground, stiffening. "Hi, I'm Lizzy."

"Child, what's become of your hair? I see no curl here nor there." She flounced Lizzy's limp strands. "No bounce or wobble, not even a spring. To whom did you lose this precious thing?" Skirts swishing, she swept behind Lizzy, tutting.

"The Shadow Rook took my curls. I had to pay him a bobby pin for saving me."

"Blood of mine paid a rook? How dare he even take a look!" Her voice turned sharp as she plucked out one of Lizzy's hairs.

"Ouch!" Lizzy grabbed her head.

"Hey, leave her alone, lady!" Marcus jumped toward Lizzy.

Eldrich pivoted. "Who's this speaking up? A knight of honor or yearling pup?" Stopping short, she looked at Marcus, her boot tapping.

"Name's Brocket. That's my friend, so keep your hands off her."

"Ah! I see, but knights don't run, so you must be the latter one," Eldrich quipped.

How did she know Marcus was a runner? Could she read their minds?

"Huh?" Marcus scratched his head.

Lizzy chimed in. "Eldrich?"

"Yes, my darling dear?"

"We have a message for you. Fas needs your help," Lizzy said.

"What would *you* ask of me?" Eldrich levitated mid-air, then sat, legs crossed.

Fairday shot Lizzy a look of warning. They had to be careful.

Lizzy caught it. "*Fas* said you're the only one who can stop a bookworm."

"Ah, I see. The favor's for him and not for thee." Eldrich twirled a curl.

"I mean, we'd also like your help." Lizzy shrugged at her partners.

"Who's we? You three?" Eldrich pointed a gloved finger at each of them.

Fairday spoke before she knew what she was saying. "We three you see, beg for Fas, this of thee." *Where did that come from?* Did it have something to do with being a Wordcaster? Or was her brain so saturated with stories, it knew how to deal with these types of situations?

Eldrich's smile stretched at the corners. Wiggling fingers, she ruffled her skirt, eyes on Fairday. "Girl's clever, but can she play? I've my doubts from what they say. Guess right, and I'm wrong. What goes by fast but is much too long?"

Fairday knew Eldrich was trying to make her question her own instincts. Considering the puzzle, she racked her brain. Could it be a snake? Or a fire hose? No, those weren't right. What answer was the Myxtress looking for? Even though her mind was racing, it felt like everything was moving at a snail's pace. *Wait. What did she just think?* The thought sparked an idea, and Fairday said the answer. "Time is what you seek."

"And so it is, until you're dead, for it only ticks inside your head," Eldrich recited.

"Will you help us then?" Lizzy asked.

Eldrich leaped in the air and landed in a pirouette. "Boon granted! More than fair. But first we fix your *dreadful* hair." Holding out a hand, she blew sparkling powder into Lizzy's face.

Lizzy jumped, then touched her head, feeling the bounce. "My curls! Oh, thank you!"

"How're we going to get to the Talking Library?" Marcus asked.

All three looked at Eldrich. She hummed and twisted a blonde lock. Staring back at them, she said, "I can't say where to go; I wasn't shown, so I don't know."

186

"What should we do?" Lizzy asked.

"We can't go through the hatch, that'll take forever," Fairday said.

"What about going around the outside again?" Marcus said.

"That's too far." Lizzy flipped her hair.

"Hey, is that Sanir?" Marcus pointed to Fairday's pack.

The spider sprang into action. He scurried up Lizzy's leg, then onto her shoulder.

Lizzy froze as he crept next to her ear, whistling and clicking. Her face lit up. "Sanir just told me how to find the portal!"

"Where?" Marcus asked.

"Follow me." Lizzy turned to leave.

"Wait," Fairday said. "What about Eldrich? My parents *cannot* see her."

Eldrich snapped her fingers, transforming into a twinkling cloud hovering over them.

"Well, alright then," Fairday said and followed her friends out.

Lizzy led them down to Thurston's study; Fairday could feel her stomach swirling. Was it a good idea to bring Eldrich to the Talking Library? What if Ruby was right, and she was behind it all? *Maybe the bookworm worked for her!* Fas said she was the only one who understood the magic. What were the odds Eldrich was even on their side?

~ Thirty Four ~
A WEB OF LIES

Fairday closed the door to Thurston's study; Lizzy and Marcus went to the bookcase. Eldrich floated overhead, then popped back into herself, brushing off the glitter.

Fairday pulled open the heavy drapes and joined her friends. Light streamed through the window. Eldrich wandered around and ran a gloved finger over things, tutting.

"Sanir wants us to find *The Secret Garden*." Lizzy pointed to the bookshelves.

The DMS scanned the titles. Marcus checked the top rows, Fairday the middle, and Lizzy the bottom. Divide and conquer; that was the fastest way.

"Here it is!" Marcus said, pulling out a book and handing it to Lizzy.

"Sanir says, knock on the front." Lizzy glanced at her partners.

"Go for it," Marcus said. "Let's hope the set of talking books doesn't answer."

Lizzy rapped on the worn leather cover and it flipped open. Mist poured from the pages and swirled into the room.

Eldrich snapped her fingers. In a poof she blended with the cloud—a flash of silver the only hint she was there.

"What's next?" Marcus asked.

"Sanir?" Lizzy touched her shoulder. "He's gone!"

"Do you think this is another setup?" Fairday raised an eyebrow.

"I *knew* I didn't trust that kid." Marcus shook his head.

"Marcus! We don't know that's true," Lizzy said, grabbing his arm, then Fairday's. "Let's stick together, maybe this is how the portal opens."

The book levitated, facing them. Fairday tried to read the words, but the sentences sank into the white spaces. Suddenly, the pages sucked the fog up like a vacuum. Fairday turned to her friends, but they'd vanished. Looking at her hands, she saw only sparkling dust. They'd all become mist! Letting the sensation sweep her into the story, Fairday remembered Larry's words: "Truth lies betwixt the lines."

The next thing Fairday knew, she was in the room out-side the Talking Library. Lizzy and Marcus stood by her side. The crystals on the chandelier tinkled as Eldrich breezed by them.

"Where's Sanir?" Lizzy glanced around the table.

"I'm here," a small voice said from the shadows.

Sanir shifted into the light. Fairday thought he looked beat up. His cloak was torn, and his ponytail was a mess. He sat down in Fas's chair and hung his head. "We need to talk."

"Ah! I see! The spider's spun lies. Don't be taken by surprise!" Eldrich said and cackled herself into a midair backflip.

"What does she mean?" Fairday asked. Sanir did look guilty. Sliding into the chairs they'd claimed the last time, the DMS waited for an answer.

"I—I—" He put his head down on the table. "It was me. I let the bookworm in."

"Why would you do that?" Lizzy asked, eyes wide.

"Do you *know* how lonely it is here?" Sanir threw his arms over the table. "I have no friends, and I never do anything except read and write. Nothing *ever* changes. Plus my father's been ignoring me since the House-keeper problem. He's always too busy with work."

Fairday hadn't thought about that, only how amazing it would be to live in a magical library. She couldn't imagine being bored! But there were two sides to every story.

"How does letting a bookworm in get you friends?" Marcus raised his eyebrows.

"I thought if someone else took over, then we'd leave and start a new life. The bookworm wanted to be the Librarian, so I didn't think it'd be a big deal. But now he's kidnapped my father and taken over the library, and it's all my fault." Sanir groaned.

Eldrich patted a yawn and fell into the empty chair. "A sad story, my young son. I hoped you'd be *loads* more fun." Standing up, she sauntered to the door. "Take us in to have a look. I've a debt to collect from a shady rook." She winked at Lizzy and twirled a curl.

~ Thirty Five ~
A CLEAR REFLECTION

Sanir brought them into the Talking Library. The only light seemed to come from the hearth in the center. They crept along the walls in the bookshelves' shadows, keeping an eye out for the poisonous punctuation. Fairday could see a figure across the room, but it was too dark and too far away to make out who it was. Eldrich slid up to them wearing a cheeky grin, and pointed to the fireplace. *Poof!* She disappeared.

"Oh my gosh!" Lizzy whispered, holding a hand to her mouth.

"What?" Marcus strained to see what it was.

"Look into the fire," Lizzy said.

Behind the flames, Fairday could see the room reflected in the mirror—*it hadn't been there before!* Did Eldrich put a charm on it? The Myxtress leaned against the hearth, stroking a book on the mantel. It was USEFUL! Richard Bittner sat at Fas's desk, bent over a book. Picking up the feather quill, he dipped it in the crystal jar of ink, then put the tip to his tongue.

"What's he doing?" Lizzy asked.

"It looks like he's licking ink," Marcus said.

"Or slurping up words," Fairday said.

"Bittner *is* the bookworm," Lizzy whispered to her partners. "But how'd he get here?"

They all looked at Sanir, waiting for an answer.

"I placed an ad in the *Ashpot Weekly* for a new Librarian." Sanir shrugged.

"How were you able to take out a classified ad?" Lizzy asked.

"I don't know. I figured it out, like how I sent the notes to you, Fairday."

"But how'd you get the reporter here?" Marcus asked.

"I just showed him. That's all." Sanir shuffled his feet.

"What do you mean?" Marcus pressed him.

"You can get here through the pages of any book if a Wordweaver gives you the title of a cover to knock on. I'm the next in line to be the Librarian. I know how the portals work."

"Wait. What?" Fairday stopped him. "Why would you lead us down that awful hatch if that's true? What was the point of figuring out the password if we could just knock on a book?"

"I'm forbidden from telling *any* human how to enter the Talking Library," Sanir said.

"But you're doing it all over the place," Lizzy pointed out.

"I know, and it's a huge problem." Sanir's eyes shifted. "My father needed your help finding Eldrich and sent me to deliver his message. He had no clue how the bookworm got into the library. I couldn't tell him *I'd* spilled our secret. Things were a mess after the House-keeper left, so I brought you in the official way, passing through Nowhere to solve the challenge."

"Why do you call Richard Bittner a bookworm?" Fairday asked.

"He drank the ink. That's what he is now."

"Drank the ink?" Marcus made a face. "Did it turn him into a monster?"

"Kind of." Sanir rubbed his chin. "It's in his blood, and words give him power. He went crazy after I let him in. He made a deal with the Shadow Rook. Together, they captured my father, then moved into the library. You must have felt it? The whole place shook."

"The earthquake was Bittner taking control of the Talking Library?"

"Yes, and the situation is getting worse. It's been ter-rible for the books." Sanir grimaced.

195

"What's *worse* than their words being eaten?" Fairday asked.

Sanir stared at his hands. "He sends their characters to Limbo."

"Limbo? What's that?" Marcus asked.

"It's where characters go once they've been removed from a story."

"How do they get there?"

"The Shadow Rook sucks them into his smoke, then brings them through the reflection in the fireplace. That's where Limbo is—behind the flames."

"What happens once they're there?" Fairday asked. *How bad could it be?*

"It's not pretty." Sanir shook his head. "After the Rook drops them off, the one-eyed purpose eater drains their story, watching them search hopelessly for new roles to play."

"I think we saw that going on behind the blinds!" Fairday remembered.

"Right! You said there was a giant eye." Lizzy flipped her hair.

"That's him." Sanir nodded. "The purpose eater is how the bookworm's getting characters to work for him.

He threatens to send them to Limbo, where they'll lose their lines."

The darkness shifted and a snake-like voice spoke up. "So we meet again, *thieves.*"

The Shadow Rook! They'd been discovered. Fairday stole a glance at the fireplace. Eldrich and USEFUL had vanished. Would she come to their rescue? Or was the Myxtress working for the bookworm? They were about to find out!

~ Thirty Six ~
SHADOWS BY LIGHT

Lizzy shrieked. Fairday felt something grip her arm. Darkness latched onto them, then shoved all four kids forward into the middle of the room. Bittner looked up from the desk, tip to tongue.

"Thieves in the library, caught skulking around," the Shadow Rook hissed.

"Not too impressed with your, uh, security, Rooky." Bittner frowned.

"They had help from the boy."

"That sniveling spider! I thought we'd, uh, chased him off." Bittner dropped the quill on the desk and picked up a book. Punching the cover, he said, "Sikes! Get out here."

Fairday shuddered. *He was not nice to books!* The cover opened and pages flew out, then formed a figure; only this time it wasn't Alice. The living sentences took the shape of a man. Bittner dipped the quill into the ink and touched a fluid word on him. Fleshy color filled the spaces between the lines, making the *papier-mâché* person appear almost real.

"Whadda ya want now?" the man grumbled, scratching his cap.

Fairday's heart jumped when she saw the mark on his back, and she whispered to Lizzy, "That's who was in the mirror, kidnapping Fas!" It hadn't been a tattoo she'd seen—it was words!

"It's Bill Sikes from *Oliver Twist*," Lizzy said behind her palm.

"Bring me Fas, dimwit." Bittner flashed a black tongue. "Tell him I've caught his, uh, boy. That'll get him to reveal where I can find the, uh, *Book of Ends*."

Lizzy grabbed Fairday's arm as Sikes strode off down a hall. "Didn't you say that title was missing from Thurston's collection? Wonder why he wants it?"

"Silence!" the Shadow Rook bellowed before Fairday could answer.

Lizzy shut her mouth as he loomed over her like black smoke.

Marcus struggled against the shady arm.

The Shadow Rook laughed. "Strength can't beat shadows, boy."

"Ah, I see! That's up to me!" Eldrich spun out of the fireplace into a curtsy.

The darkness creeping over Lizzy pulled back, and the Shadow Rook retreated.

Bittner was confused. Fairday didn't think he knew about Eldrich. If the Shadow Rook was no match for her, then it should be a snap to get rid of a bookworm.

Eldrich's skirts spun as she circled the Rook, backing him up to the false flames.

"Heard you stole my family look. A bobby pin is what you took." She held out her hand.

A flash of light lit up his form, and he produced Lizzy's bobby pin.

Eldrich plucked it from his dark palm; her rosy face turned grim. "*This* Rook plays a dirty game, hard to lose, such a shame." Tutting, she stuck the pin into her curls and glanced at Lizzy. "You helped the girl for your gain, but switching sides is such a pain." She turned a sharp eye on him. Her voice echoed through the library as she pointed to the Shadow Rook. "Stay in rank, that's the rule, even when cast a fool." Eldrich raised her arms.

"Wait!" The Shadow Rook cowered under her stare.

"Shadows by light, remove this traitor from my sight." A glowing ball of light formed in Eldrich's hands, and she threw it at him.

The Shadow Rook burst into a puff of smoke up the chimney, and Eldrich spun on her heels. Fairday glanced at Fas's desk. *Oh no!* Bittner had left. She looked around, but couldn't spot him anywhere. "Hey! He's gone."

"Over there!" Marcus pointed across the room.

Bittner turned down an aisle, trying to get away. Suddenly, the shelves tipped, and books rained down on his head. Fairday saw **HARMFUL** perched on top of the pile, ruffling his pages. USEFUL was next to him, sporting a wide grin, and *Interesting* popped in from nowhere, eyes spinning. Books had beaten the bookworm!

Thirty Seven
BOOK BINDINGS

Fas was pushed into the room by a grumbling Bill Sikes. The Librarian was tied up, arms tight by his sides. Sikes seemed to realize something was off and stopped in his tracks.

"Get them!" Bittner scrambled over flapping books.

"What?" Sikes stood motionless. His eyes shifted from Bittner to Fas.

Fairday couldn't guess his thoughts. Was Sikes trying to decide which side he was on? She crossed her fingers and hoped he'd make the right choice in *this* scene.

Scratching his head, Sikes untied the rope and set Fas free. The Librarian's violet eyes lit up and he pointed. Threads shot out from his hand and tied up Bittner. Fas then turned to Sikes and touched him; pages fell to the floor.

Eldrich waggled a finger. Bittner spun into the air and landed on the couch. Fas strode over to them and Sanir ran into his father's arms.

"I'm sorry." He hung his head. "I messed up, and it's all my fault."

"I know what you did," Fas said, looking down at his son. "I forgive you, but you *will* be held accountable for your actions, you understand that."

"I get it." Sanir shuffled his feet.

"Now, I'd like you to go to your room, so I can finish this business and see our guests off. We'll discuss this later, son." Fas patted his arm.

Turning to face the DMS, Sanir said, "Thank you for helping me save my father. I won't forget it."

"We're glad it worked out." Lizzy flipped her curls.

Eldrich tutted at him, watching Lizzy with keen approval.

"Yeah, great that you're home." Fairday smiled.

"Catch ya later, dude," Marcus said.

Sanir left the room, and Fas fixed his gaze on the bookworm.

Bittner squirmed on the couch. "Well, seems the, uh, shoe's on the other foot." He flicked his tongue.

"It certainly does. Your hunt for the *Book of Ends* is over. You'll never get your hands on it. You drank library ink—your life belongs to books now," Fas said. "You must be bound."

Eldrich spun on her heels. "Ah, I see, a good ole book-binding it's to be!"

"Bound?" Bittner's eyes widened. "You mean, uh, like a book?"

Fairday could see sweat beading on Bittner's brow. His black tongue lashed at the corners of his mouth as he struggled to get loose.

"Yes," Fas answered with a solemn nod. "I'm afraid you made your choice when you agreed to the terms of my job."

"Whadda ya mean, terms?"

"Rule one, if the Librarian ever drinks ink from the Talking Library, they shall be bound to a book to live by the lines of its story."

Bittner's eyes bulged under his baseball cap. "It's just ink. Who cares if I drank a few lousy drops? I won't tell anyone if you, uh, let me go."

"Ah, I see! *This* worm thinks we'll set him free!" Eldrich giggled and twirled a curl.

"Why *do* you eat words?" Marcus asked.

Bittner turned to him. "Why not?" He flicked his tongue.

"Because they're not food, so what's the point?"

"Kid's got moxie." Bittner nodded. "Here's the point"—he licked his lips—"because they, uh, give me power, and there ain't nothin' sweeter than that."

"You don't seem very powerful now." Fairday pointed out.

Eldrich cackled and spun on her boots.

"Why were you snooping around the Begonia House?" Lizzy asked.

"Had to." His voice was deflated. "Trying to catch the, uh, spider."

"So *you* left the note in my Harry Potter book?" Fairday asked, feeling anger rising. He'd snuck into her bedroom! That was totally unacceptable. She glared at him.

Bittner faked a laugh. "Just a joke! Didn't want you kids getting in the, uh, way."

"How'd you know we were looking for the Odds?" Marcus asked.

"Hehehe." Bittner flicked his tongue. "You might say I was keeping, uh, eyes on you."

"What does *that* mean?" Lizzy asked.

A question mark dragonfly landed on Fairday's shoulder.

"There's your, uh, answer." Bittner nodded as it buzzed off.

"You mean, the punctuation's been spying on us?" Lizzy's eyes widened.

"Yes, ma'am." He flicked his tongue, grinning.

"Why were you trying to find the *Book of Ends?*" Fairday asked.

"If I'd found it, things would've turned out, uh, different."

Fairday shuddered. *What did that mean?*

"But you didn't." Fas stood and came around the desk, cloak trailing in his wake.

Eldrich slid up next to him, and they fixed their sights on Bittner. He shrank back, eyes pinging from one to the other. *Were they really going to bind him to a book?*

Fas nodded at Eldrich, and she flew up. Flexing her fingers, she pointed at Bittner and cast the spell. "By this book, ye are bound. On this page, ye are found. Ink flows in your spine, binding you to words in line." The wind in the room kicked up like a tornado.

Fas held a book open toward Bittner—its pages flipped wildly. When they stopped, Bittner popped out of the scene. He was gone. The Librarian closed the cover, and the bookworm was no more.

~ Thirty Eight ~
WHICH SIDE?

"Where'd Bittner go?" Fairday asked, glancing around. He was nowhere to be seen.

"He's part of this story now." Fas sat down and placed the book in his desk drawer.

"Can he ever escape?" Marcus raised his eyebrows.

"Not unless the spine cracks." Fas leaned back in his chair and touched the tips of his fingers. "You three rose to the challenge. Impressive."

"It wasn't easy." Marcus puffed out his chest. "But our detective skills are off the charts."

"Are the words the bookworm ate *really* gone?" Fairday asked.

"No, now that he's been bookbound, the damage will be reversed."

"What'll happen to the characters he sent to Limbo?"

"They'll be returned to their stories. All will be set back in order."

"But how will you get another Housekeeper for the library?" Even though Fairday loved books, there was *no way* she was volunteering. She didn't want to spend the rest of her life living in a memory. Who would take Ruby's place on the other side?

"*That* girl was a sour grape." Eldrich rolled her eyes. "Of course, she wasn't in ripe shape." She howled and slapped her knee.

Fas faced Eldrich. "What you did to Ruby was cruel, even for you."

Eldrich's eyes became slits, and she waggled a finger at him. "Thurston Begonia made the deal. *He* chose to cheat and steal."

Fas watched her closely. "His debt did not include his daughter. That was not *our* initial agreement to find a Housekeeper." He leaned forward on the desk, folding his hands.

Eldrich's eyes shifted. "Well, who's to say this or that, it's not a game of tit for tat."

"No, but we are missing a player." Fas turned his attention on the DMS. "As you know, the Talking Library *must* have a Housekeeper to keep the ink to the library flowing."

"Where'll you find someone to take *that* job?" Marcus asked.

"Under normal conditions, the role of Housekeeper is passed down to a member of one of the five ancient families that inherit the responsibility. The manner in which Ruby filled the position broke tradition, but nevertheless it happened, and I had to deal with it. As all debts are cancelled regarding this matter now, I should be able to find someone to replace Ruby. There are many people who'd choose to live in a memory, and you can find anything at the Master's Emporium."

They'd found a key to the Master's Emporium— whatever that was! Fairday glanced at Lizzy, thinking she'd be making the same connection, but instead Lizzy was frowning at Eldrich.

"If it's no trouble to get a Housekeeper, then why did you do that to Ruby?" Lizzy asked. Fairday could tell her friend didn't want Eldrich to be bad. *They were so alike!* Eldrich didn't answer. She twirled a curl and looked the other way.

Fas spoke up. "She wanted revenge, that's why." He stood and went to the fireplace. Eldrich poked at a period creeping along the mantel. He continued, "When the blueprints were delivered to Thurston, he agreed to be the Housekeeper. He'd made the arrangement with Eldrich to save his wife, Cora Lynn, who was ill. Living in a memory would have cured her. But Cora Lynn was pregnant, and she refused to go to the other side of the Begonia House. After she died, Thurston was bereft with grief and wouldn't fulfill his end of the deal." Fas shook his head and clasped his hands behind his cloak.

Fairday could understand why Thurston didn't follow through with the bargain, given the circumstances, but it probably wasn't easy to break a contract with a Myxtress.

Eldrich tutted like she'd heard Fairday's thoughts.

"Years later, Eldrich tricked Ruby because of Thurston's poor choice not to pay her what she was owed."

"Ah, I see! Fas *thinks* he knows me." Eldrich waggled a finger in the air.

Marcus scratched his head. "But then who was the Housekeeper the whole time Ruby was growing up? She was eighteen when she disappeared on her wedding day."

Marcus's memory was spot on—it was a good point. Eighteen years *was* a long time. Wouldn't the ink have run out?

"There was a temporary arrangement in place during that time." Fas lowered his eyes. "But that is a sad tale, and not meant to be told now."

Eldrich glowered at him. "Like father, like son—not telling us all the lies he's spun."

Fas shot her a warning look. Eldrich tutted and rolled her eyes.

"Whose side are you on anyway?" Fairday asked Eldrich. She had to know.

The Myxtress faced Fairday and held out the palm of her hand. "*This* girl believes in sides, but good and bad are changing tides."

"That doesn't answer the question." Lizzy flipped her hair.

Eldrich's blue eyes twinkled at Lizzy. "There's a place for you in my heart, and darling dear, that's a start." She spun on her heels.

A whoosh of black feathers flew over their heads, and Edgar landed on Fas's shoulder.

"Edgar!" Fairday exclaimed. "He's yours?"

"Yes, well, he's his *own*, really." Fas rubbed the magpie's head with a finger. Edgar turned a beady eye on them, then hopped off to perch on the mantel.

"He's quite shy actually." Fas sat back at his desk. "Took me ages to convince him to talk to you, even after Sikes caught me. But he came around, didn't you, old boy?" Edgar cawed and ruffled his feathers.

The stone king and queen shifted to the side as Fas led the children to the passage behind the fireplace. Fairday could hear birds chirping and smell the earthy scent of the woods. They were almost home! Eldrich skipped ahead as they said goodbye to Fas.

"Tell Sanir we'll keep in touch," Lizzy said.

"He'll be happy to hear that. Sanir would benefit from having a few good friends. It will make it easier for him to accept his place as the next Librarian." Fas placed his hand over his heart. "The stories thank you, and so do I." Bowing to Fairday, he added, "A Wordcaster is always welcome in the Talking Library. If it weren't for your kind, my job would be boring."

"Thanks," Fairday said, smiling. She didn't know what to say. That was possibly the greatest invitation she'd ever gotten.

Following behind Lizzy, Fairday went through the fireplace, anxious to be on the path to the other side of her house. How long were they gone? She didn't want to be late for her party!

The trio waved goodbye to Eldrich from the front porch. The Myxtress stood back and faced them with her arms

raised. She chanted words they couldn't hear, then spun on her heels. *Poof!* she disappeared.

"That's what she did when Ruby thought she'd cursed the house." Fairday's stomach twisted in a knot. "You don't think that's what she's doing now, do you?"

"Nope. I can tell she likes me." Lizzy blushed. "I mean, Eldrich did some things in the past that could be seen as cruel, but I don't think she wants to hurt us."

"Who knows, maybe she's finally taking that curse off?" Marcus said.

Fairday let her friends' words put her at ease. There was no use worrying about it now, not when the bookworm had been stopped, and stories were in order. It was time to see what was waiting for them on *her* side of the Begonia House.

~ Thirty Nine ~
A GATHERING OF CHARACTERS

The girls put on their costumes in Fairday's bedroom. Now that the case was solved and books were safe from the bookworm, they were excited for the party to start and checked their looks in the mirror.

"That case was insane." Lizzy pushed her blonde curls back in a black headband. Turning to Fairday, she curtsied. In the sky blue dress and white pinafore, she was clearly Alice.

"You're getting good at that." Fairday clicked her silver shoes. She'd traded her ponytail for two braids, and they hung down as she picked up a basket.

"You betcha! Runs in the family." Lizzy twirled a curl.

"Thank goodness we got back in time," Fairday said and picked up a pair of red slippers, then popped them into the basket. She'd put them on later to be Dorothy from the movie.

"After what we've been dealing with, I'm looking forward to a good scream," Lizzy said. "I'd bet my Halloween candy your dad's haunted parlor will do the trick."

Walking into the hall, they saw Marcus, whose orange Camp Half-Blood shirt and homemade goat feet screamed Grover from *The Lightning Thief.* Fairday loved it! She couldn't wait to see what other characters showed up at the Halloween party.

Loud moans and chains crashing made all three of them jump.

"Where'd your parents get a soundtrack like *this*?" Marcus asked.

"My dad spent weeks mixing it. He's been stalking me, saying things like, 'True fright grips all your senses,' and 'Leave 'em screaming, they'll come back.'" Fairday rolled her eyes.

Flashing lights lit up cobwebs spun around the chandelier, and the Bride of Frankenstein, aka Pru Morrow, stirred a cauldron oozing green haze at the bottom of the stairs. A graveyard had sprung up on the black-and-white floor, and a skeleton hung from a coffin by the front doors. The Begonia House *was* spooky, but it would never look more like a haunted house than this!

Auntie Em waddled up to them, nudging Fairday's leg. "Look at you! Cutest Cowardly Lion ever!" Fairday scratched the pug's head. This was the last anyone would see of Auntie Em for the night. Once guests started arriving, the little dog's character would come through.

Frankenstein ushered a group of kids into the parlor. Everyone was laughing and pointing, checking out the house they'd heard so many stories about. Fairday noticed Olivia walking wide eyed through the foyer. Her blonde hair was tucked under a witch's hat with a lion on it, and she wore a Ravenclaw cloak; she was clearly Luna Lovegood. A kid with an orange jumpsuit came in, and Fairday noticed the back said Camp Green Lake. He had a fake shovel and a pair of gold sneakers around his neck. Stanley Yelnats from *Holes*. Awesome! The boy turned and Fairday saw it was Dif. He looked different without his skull-and-crossbones jacket. Maybe there was more to him than she thought. They liked the same book after all.

After a round of pumpkin bowling in the parlor, Fairday needed some punch. Lizzy and Marcus had the same idea, and the three friends walked to the table. They were surprised when the Grim Reaper turned around and Larry Lovell's blue eyes looked back at them.

Larry cleared his throat. "Hm, mm. You didn't think I'd miss your party did you, Miss Morrow?" He raised an eyebrow. "When your parents asked me to help out, it seemed like the perfect opportunity." Leaning in, he whispered, "Any news about Bittner and that bookworm?"

Fairday, Lizzy, and Marcus filled Larry in about what had happened in the Talking Library, trying not to leave out too many details.

"Bittner was the bookworm." Larry scratched his chin. "I can't say I'll miss his reports; sounds like he'll have to stick to his story now." He tapped his scythe on the floor.

Marcus burst out laughing. "That was the best joke ever."

The Grim Reaper winked at him, then glided away, cloak billowing.

"So, what do you guys think about the Master's Emporium?" Fairday bit her thumbnail.

"I wonder what it is?" Lizzy asked.

"No clue," Marcus shrugged.

"I've heard of it," a gruff voice said, pushing by Marcus to grab the punch ladle.

Fairday looked to see who it was. Stanley Yelnats, otherwise known as *Dif!*

Marcus planted his hooves on the floor. "What do you know about it?"

"Plenty." Dif slugged back a cup of punch. Picking up his shovel, he turned to Fairday. "Can I talk to you later?" He fixed his eyes on Marcus as he added, "In private."

"Dude, you have to come and touch these eyeballs. They are *so* gross." Bart came up from behind. Fairday thought his costume was fitting: Dudley Dursley. Perfect.

Dif nodded at Fairday, mouthing, "Talk to you later," before heading off with Bart.

"Well, that was an interesting turn of events," Lizzy said, eyes wide.

"Wonder what Dif knows about the Master's Emporium?" Marcus rubbed his chin.

"Who knows! I bet we'll find out though," Fairday said. "But now it sounds like we should get in there and touch those eyeballs!"

Mr. and Mrs. Morrow had thought of everything. The spooktacularness *had* made the kids oooh and aaahh, and Fairday felt proud. After cake was served and wolfed down, the guests thinned out.

"Epic party." Marcus gathered his bags. "Kids are gonna be talking about it for ages."

"You betcha!" Lizzy beamed.

"Hey, guys." Fairday huddled in close to her friends. "I have some news."

"What?" Lizzy asked.

"Dif wants to join the DMS." Fairday twisted her ponytail.

"He wants in?" Marcus raised his eyebrows. "How does he even know about it?"

"Yep. He heard us talking. I told him I'd discuss it with you guys, then let him know," Fairday said. "He seems nicer, but do you think it's a good idea to trust him?"

"Even if he gets the riddle, what about his character?" Marcus started pacing. "I've known him a lot longer than you two, and I'm not so sure."

"I know what you're saying. But people can change if they want to. He came as Stanley Yelnats. That's got to be a good sign," Fairday said. Was she plugging for him? *Weird.*

"That is a point. Plus, with all the shady people we've been meeting, maybe we could use someone who knows how to be tough." Lizzy shrugged.

"He did say he's heard of the Master's Emporium. He might have information that'll get us started on the next case," Fairday said.

"My brain is toast after solving this mystery. I can't decide right now." Marcus scratched his head. "Let's think about it and see how he is at school."

"Agreed," Lizzy and Fairday said in unison.

Lights pulled into the driveway and Marcus picked up his stuff. Fairday's parents, aka the Frankensteins, came over to say goodbye.

Marcus thanked them, then nodded at the girls. "Catch you later."

"Bye, Marcus. See you Monday." Fairday clicked her ruby slippers.

"Later, Brocket." Lizzy gave him a curtsy.

Marcus winked, then hopped down the steps.

Lizzy snored lightly, and Fairday snuggled into her sleeping bag. She hadn't been able to rest easy in the Begonia House, but she knew tonight would be different. The stories she loved were safe. The DMS had solved the case of the Talking Library, and the gathering of characters at her party had been a success. Fairday closed her eyes, letting sleep set the sails and take her away, wondering what the next mystery would be.

ACKNOWLEDGMENTS

Writing the second book in the Fairday Morrow series had many twists in the road, and we learned more than we ever expected.

Our agent, Gina Panettieri, from Talcott Notch Literary helped us stay on track. Her knowledge, suggestions, and support gave us the confidence we needed to move forward with this project and bring it to completion.

What makes this book truly special is that not only did we get to write it together, but the illustrations took the mystery to the next level, and they were created by our close friend, David SanAngelo. We've been fans of his since our teenage years in high school. Having his brilliance touch the story brought the scenes to life, and it was an amazing experience working with such a talented illustrator.

Editors are special people because they help make writing sparkle. We don't know what we would have done without the expertise of Betsy Thorpe and Nicole Ayers. You both taught us about the important things to include in the story and the correct rules to follow. The book became stronger with each revision. Thank you for your tenacity, patience, and insight.

Every step of a book's birth is complex. We could not have produced such a beautiful cover and interior without the skilled hands of Chris Robinson. He did a wonderful job laying out the design.

Our family and friends have been a strong line of support throughout the process of writing this book. It's been a labor of love bringing the next case in the DMS files into the world, but the story would not be what it is today without those who helped along the way.

Thank you to all the schools, libraries, stores, restaurants, and bookstores that invited us to talk about our journey. We enjoyed spending time with you and sharing our advice on crafting a story. All of the people we've encountered along the way have been an inspiration.

We've also found a nice group of book buddies online. Connecting with bloggers around the world has been fascinating and it's linked our world together. We appreciate the support we've received on the web from our friends around the book block.

A special thank you to Ron and James for their constant love and support during our editing days. We know it wasn't easy! It's been a long and winding road, and you've helped us get to where we are today.

Lastly, thank you to the best co-author anyone could ever ask for. Anything's possible!

ABOUT THE AUTHORS

Jessica Haight is a true New Englander, with a deep desire to be near the ocean and a love of the four seasons. She is delighted to be creating stories with her close friends, Stephanie and David. Jessica enjoys drawing while standing up and cultivating magic in her garden. She easily floats away in the pages of a good story and is still waiting for her owl from Hogwarts. Jessica lives in Connecticut with her family.

Stephanie Robinson lives with her husband in a quiet town, though it is not as quaint as Ashpot. After teaching fifth grade for almost fifteen years, she is now enjoying her role as a school media specialist. One of the many benefits of her job is that she learns something new every day. When Stephanie isn't working, she spends her time creating stories, getting lost in books, and traveling to new places.

ABOUT THE ILLUSTRATOR

David SanAngelo is an award winning illustrator, a two-time Emmy nominated director of animated shows for children and he won a kite flying contest in the fourth grade. Dave attended high school with Jessica and Stephanie and they've all been friends for a billion years. Some of Dave's favorite things are: old monster movies, superheroes and shred-a-licious rock music. Although he grew up in New England, Dave currently lives with his wife and sons in Decatur, GA.